Two Moons in August

Two Moons in August

A NOVEL BY

MARTHA BROOKS

Little, Brown and Company

Boston   New York   Toronto   London

First U.S. Edition 1992

The characters and events portrayed in this book are fictitious. Any similarity to real persons, living or dead, is coincidental and not intended by the author.

Library of Congress Cataloging-in-Publication Data

Brooks, Martha, 1944–
    Two moons in august : a novel / by Martha Brooks. — 1st ed.
        p.   cm.
    Summary: Kieran, a new boy visiting her small town for the summer, helps Sidonie and her family come together again following the death of Sidonie's mother.
    ISBN 0-316-10979-7
    [1. Death — Fiction.   2. Family problems — Fiction.
    3. Friendship — Fiction.]   I. Title.
    PZ7.B79750n   1992
    [Fic] — dc20   91-22956

10 9 8 7 6 5 4 3

MV-NY

Printed in the United States of America

For my mother

and for Maureen Hunter

The author gratefully acknowledges the Manitoba Arts Council for financial assistance; George Toles, Maureen Hunter, Alice Drader, and editors Shelley Tanaka and Melanie Kroupa for their fine advice and encouragement; and Kirsten Brooks for the gift of her wisdom and honesty during the final stages of this book.

Two Moons in August

1 —◎—

Our Angel Mother, who art in Heaven, flapping around with both sets of grandparents, used to say my hair is just like Lucille's. That's her sister who lives in the States, in Cincinnati. We have never actually met Auntie Lucille. She is supposed to be the beauty of the family. Although, like Auntie Monique, she never got married.

Mom's hair was black — like mine — but straight. I combed it for her the morning of the day she died, almost a year ago now. Nineteen fifty-nine has actually been a pretty good year so far. Nothing terrible has happened. Yet.

"Put on some Coppertone," says Roberta, holding the bottle out to me. "There's a glare on the water. You'll burn yourself."

"Good," I say, running for the lake. "After I burn again, it'll turn into a really impressive tan."

"Sidonie! Sid-on-*ee* — you'll make yourself sick!"

"Drop dead, Bobbi," I say, sinking up to my shoulders in the water.

Behind me, she heaves one of her sighs. "Fine then, *kiddo*, ignore me."

"Thanks, I will." I stand up and half wade, half run, farther into the lake to get away from her.

My sister is home for the summer from university. She is nineteen, a strawberry blond, and she doesn't want to be called Bobbi anymore now that she's decided to become a pediatrician. I told her that I don't want to be called kiddo anymore, either. She says she just calls me that sometimes because I am a kid. (*Her* opinion.)

I can hardly wait to get my driver's license. Then we'll see how she enjoys sharing the car keys.

I was named Sidonie after our French grandmother. It's kind of a strange name, but you get used to it.

Our valley is called Bison Valley. The lake floats in its belly. The Assiniboine and Chippewa hunted and killed buffalo here. This whole valley is lousy with the spirits of those who have passed on. Dad's a doctor on staff here where we live, close to the U.S. border, in the province's largest TB (which means tuberculosis) sanatorium. Some of the lives the doctors save. Others, they don't.

Bobbi was seven and I was three when Mom became sick. We all moved here, to be closer to her. She'd always been frail, Dad said, and that's why we stayed on in the country after she recovered from TB. They say fresh air is supposed to be good for frail people.

I guess it doesn't matter, after it's all over, how a person died, except to those who remember them and didn't want to lose them in the first place. Mom died of heart failure. Her heart stopped the day I turned fifteen.

I am exactly two and a half weeks away from my sixteenth birthday. One of these days Bobbi is going to have to realize that the kiddo aspect of me got the ax a year ago, and maybe then she'll back off.

Today the lake smells fishy and is warm as a bathtub. It's always like this halfway through summer. Dead minnows mixed with seaweed, shale, and foam wash up against the shore; horseflies zoom around in the clammy air, but I love this lake. And I always will.

In the boathouse there is this heavy wide-bottomed sailboat that Dad built for Mom and now refuses to have anything to do with. Two or three times a summer, when she was well, we'd all pile in, sail in the afternoon breezes down to the end of the lake, have a picnic, and then come floating back at night. Under the full bright moon, owls would hoot at us from the valley hillsides. There's this spooky legend about how each month they come to call somebody's spirit away. But we'd laugh as Dad would stand up perfectly straight in the boat, put his hands around his mouth, and hoot back, just to confuse them.

I can't swim, but this lake wraps around me like a worn old blanket. That is, when I'm close to shore.

Slowly I test the depth where the lake starts to drop off, touching along the bottom until the soft silky mud sucks at my tiptoes. Water rushes up past my chin. Cripes, it's scary. Quickly going under, I kick off at the bottom. Come thrashing up with my arms rotating like a crazy person. Frantically dance back toward shore.

Finally, at a place where I can stand, I pretend-swim —

touching down to mud before kicking off, my body rising up behind. My arms stroke the surface like in an old Esther Williams movie. I am now Esther doing a synchronized swimming routine in a large Hollywood pool, surrounded by a "bevy of beauties."

Sometimes I think I'm okay to look at. Sometimes I think I'm ugly. I even go through phases where I feel there is a possibility that I will be beautiful, like Bobbi. Being small, with a long neck and pale French skin is okay, except I'd rather be taller. My eyes are large and sometimes gray and sometimes blue, depending on my mood. That's good. I have a slim nose and pouty (when I practice in front of the mirror) Brigitte Bardot lips. Not bad, either.

I have impossible hair. I hate it. It's thick and wavy. Don't believe what anybody tells you — naturally curly hair is a royal pain. When it rains, or is hot, or even sometimes when it snows, naturally curly hair is as attractive as a Brillo pad. I've practically given up on it and there's nobody around here to look at me anyway, but I keep it long to minimize the curl — just in case.

Bobbi is wearing her satiny new Jantzen bathing suit. She bought it yesterday with money from her summer job when we were doing our weekly shopping over at Crystal Lake. Her suit is black with straps that unbutton front and back. It goes well with her white skin and pale freckles. Her eyes are the same color as the green lake when light puddles on top of the water. Her straight hair never stays curled and suits her that way.

A horsefly dives at Bobbi's thin white thighs. She sits up and gives it a swat. I stand up to my waist in the glinting silty water and grin at my bobbing reflection. I pull off my

6

rubber bathing cap. It smells like old tires. I hurl it onto the shore.

It hits the legs of a tall boy who wasn't there before. Where did he come from?

He stands looking out at me and won't stop looking. He has the kind of light brown hair that bleaches in the summer, and it lies in tight flat gold-flecked curls all over his head. He's about my age. I've never seen him before in my life.

"This your beach?" He picks up my cap with long tanned fingers. His voice is low and husky.

I shrug. He just stares and stares. I want to hide. I want to appear nonchalant. "It's our boathouse," I say, trudging, head down, through the water, "but nobody owns the beach."

I look up as Roberta deadpans her flirty older woman stare and then rolls over onto her stomach. He turns his eyes back to me. I stop and raise my arms, rake down my wild sopping hair.

"You don't mind if I swim here, then?" He isn't looking at my hair.

"It's a free country." I drop my arms.

He kicks off his brown loafers — he isn't wearing socks — and next thing he's peeling off a thin white T-shirt. He drops it beside his feet, unbuttons his pale cotton pants, looks up.

I look away and pull a dragonfly off my hip. Its sticky legs dance in the air. I set it on my hand. Its wings are wet. It raises a shiny greenish blue tail and crawls like a miniature drunk up my arm. I head with it for shore as the boy dives into the water and cuts a straight clean line right

7

past me. He swims like a city boy, used to pools and lessons.

I climb onto a high rock that's flat on top and smooth as a table. It's partly shaded by an overhanging oak. I sit my bum on the cool part and let my feet blister against the rest. The dragonfly, getting more frisky, now stumbles around on my upturned legs.

Roberta turns her head, squints at me with one eye, sees I'm fine, groans, and falls back into a kind of hot, dazed oblivion.

The boy has rolled over onto his back. With a quick streak of feet and hands he glides, easy as butter, in for shore. He has a long tanned body and nice muscles — not the kind that look freakish, but the kind that just sort of hide under the surface.

He suddenly stands up, looking straight at me again as water comes sloshing over his hair, his face, his body.

I turn back to the dragonfly, which darts away over our weathered gray boathouse and on up the valley hills. I pretend not to notice as the boy moves onto the beach.

"You live around here?" He rubs his head with a flapping towel, then carelessly works it down his body.

"Yes," I say, as if he's startled me. "Up the road. At the sanatorium."

His eyes are light brown and huge as he looks up at me on the rock.

"No kidding," he says slowly. "Me, too."

I look down at my feet. Wiggle my toes. Hug my knees right up against my body.

TB patients at the sanatorium are mostly older people. Kids with TB are treated in the city. So who is this guy?

8

Dr. Elsa McMorran's son? Maybe. He's the right age. If this is the one, he's from Toronto. And his father, who's also a doctor, is still living there. So has he come to live with the mother? Or just for a visit?

I pick a piece of black shale off my baby toe. I could start up a conversation, but I haven't talked to a boy since school finished in June, and even then I wasn't ever exactly what you'd call practiced at it.

Roberta sits up and lights a cigarette. She pulls tobacco off her tongue, snaps it away, and blows out through Revlon "Torch Song Red" lips. She pulls her legs up to her chin and stares out into the water.

Sharp hot shale stings my feet as I slide from the rock. He watches me all the way over to Roberta on the dock. I fumble one of her cigarettes out of a crumpled package and scratch a match on the side of the boathouse and put the cigarette to my mouth.

She checks me over her shoulder, then the boy. Rolling her eyes, she turns back to the lake.

I blow a complicated smoke ring. I'm calm. I'm going to blow two more rings. There, one. And — two. Magically, I'm bored and sophisticated — holding the cigarette that certain way, like Marlene Dietrich did in *The Blue Angel*.

I look over to see if he's seen this, and his head does a speedy I-didn't-see-you turn away. I grind out the cigarette. I'm casual. I saunter.

Then I stumble. Flap out one hand to keep from falling flat. My hand and my knee both hit the beach. I stagger up and want to die. He's seen all this.

He's smiling. He's shaking sand out of his hair. His

swimming trunks are royal blue, a fashionable color. They fit him like a glove.

Suddenly, I feel like an old sow in my three-year-old plaid bathing suit. I wade into the lake. Sink up to my shoulders before I turn and face the shore.

He slides on his cotton pants and pulls up the zipper. He eases his feet into the leather loafers. Throws the towel around his still-wet shoulders. He flashes me a look before I can turn away.

"This what you country folks call the Old Swimming Hole?"

I turn one entire circle, scudding my hand in a bumpy way across the water. "It isn't a hole. It's a lake." Who does he think he is, anyway?

"Sure a lot of bugs and dead stuff," he says, hands hanging easy as you please on his hips. He's looking everywhere now except at me. "Guess you're used to that."

He has a slim face, a long nose, and full lips that blend with his tan.

"Lucky guess." I tip up my nose coldly. "But we enjoy the bugs. They ward off pests."

The smile he's been wearing is now fixed on his face. He stands there, not moving.

I attempt to stare him down. He blushes but keeps staring back. So I come splashing in to shore, making sure to water-spot his nice beige pants as I pass by.

I snatch up my towel. It's wet. I wipe sand and shale down my leg.

He bends, and his muscles move just below the skin of his arm. He reaches out with a one-fingered flick and sends my bathing cap flying toward me. I catch it at my knees.

He picks up his T-shirt and stuffs it partway into his back pocket. "Thanks for nothing," he says in a soft, angry voice.

I watch him climb up the trail toward the road, weaving around the tall weeds and grasses that come to his hips. I watch as the buffalo-shaped valley hills creep down around his tense bare shoulders. I watch until he's finally gone. Then I watch the top of the empty trail for a while. I wish that he'd come back.

I drop my towel and kick my way back to the water.

Roberta's snapping each red-painted fingernail — lost in her own thoughts. She sighs and shifts and slowly lowers her head until her cheek comes down on her knee. There isn't much wind. The sun-heated water tugs away at my ankles. Swish-in, swish-out, swish-in, swish-out. I feel sad and lonely, as though something has just been pulled from deep inside me.

2 ⟶◎⟶

The week that I turned eight, Mom and Bobbi and I went on a car trip to the Qu'Appelle Valley. Dad couldn't come along — we'd already been to Florida that spring. He leaned in the car window as we were leaving. "You're sure you'll be all right?"

Mom hooded her eyes with her small hand. "You're such a worrier." She smiled gaily. "Don't miss us too much!"

He stood back, never taking his eyes off her. Bobbi and I waved to him out the rear window. Mom stuck out her hand and waved, too, watching him from the car's side mirror. He kept slowly waving to her, his long arm high over his head, until we'd turned off the driveway and couldn't see him anymore.

I plunked down in the backseat and pouted. "He didn't see me."

"Of course he did," said eleven-year-old Bobbi, rolling

her eyes as if she thought I was being totally dense. "He just saw Mom more. She's his *wife!*"

Mom's oldest sister, Monique, is still the principal of a small-town school near a lake in the Qu'Appelle. We stayed with Auntie Monique for five days, picked berries or went boating in the mornings, swam in the hot afternoons, and on my birthday she made a heart-shaped cake with pink coconut icing and nine candles (one to grow on).

Mom tried to teach me how to swim. I clutched her neck. I *knew* that there were monsters deep down in the lake, watching, ready to swim up and eat my toes.

"I'm *here*, you funny monkey." She laughed, hugging me against her. Her bathing suit straps dug into her soft round shoulders. "Do you really believe," she whispered, "that I'll let you go before you're ready?"

Auntie Monique was always going to come to visit us, but somehow she never did. And the next time we saw her was at Mom's funeral. Her hair was in a bun at the back of her neck, and she was all dressed in gray except for short pure-white gloves that each did up at the wrist with a pearl.

My hands are like Mom's. Last summer we used to put them together out on the lawn cart overlooking the ravine. I'd smooth out her garden-roughened fingers, make her palm go flat and place mine on top. Then I'd dance my fingers up and down like a spider on a mirror.

"Daddy longlegs," she'd say in her tired voice. "Your fingers are Fred Astaire."

Not far behind us her prickly-stemmed roses grew all

down the sunny side of the house. Dad looks after her roses now, on Sundays, his one day at home. He spends most of his time working at the infirmary, eats practically every meal in the cafeteria, sleeps about five hours a night, honors us with his presence for about an hour each day, and basically lies to himself that life is going on the same as usual (he keeps a huge picture of Mom on his dresser).

Roberta has taken over the house (our housekeeper has been given a three-month vacation) and has also taken back her old job, from before Mom died, of cooking the meals — even though I discovered over the winter that I'm a much better cook, and she still hates cooking as much as ever.

She's come home for the summer, Dad says, "to help out in the family." Translation: to boss me around and yell at me to, "Get your nose out of that book!"

When Roberta isn't studying, she hardly ever reads real books. And she acts as if the world is coming to an end when anybody else does. Her idea of a useful summer activity is floor scrubbing.

Several times a day I bang out of the house to run under the hard blue sky with the sun so strong on my face that I can actually smell it. Sometimes, this is the only thing that keeps me from going totally insane.

Roberta's other summer job is working part-time as a ward aide in the infirmary, and that's where she met and got friendly with doctor-to-be Philip Lim, the only person who ever seems to make her happy.

Phil's minister father and mother came over to this country from China. He and his older brother grew up in the Okanagan Valley.

14

Their parents were on their way to church one Sunday morning when a big fruit truck pulled out of a side road and plowed into them, sending them out of this world so fast it'd make your head spin. Phil wasn't with them because that was the year, at the age of fifteen, that he rebelled and decided he wasn't going to church anymore.

The brother wasn't there either, because at the time he was in Toronto setting up his medical practice. After the funeral, Phil went to live with him.

He told me all this on one of those rare nights this summer when he came over to our house and Roberta wasn't waiting for him.

I'd been sitting in front of the TV, loosely braiding my cat's whiskers.

There was a little rat-a-tat on the wooden frame of the back screen door. I jumped off the sofa, expecting Phil's voice to echo in right away from the kitchen. But he rapped again as I got there.

I whipped open the door. "Hi!"

He just stood there — skinny and tall under the amber back-door light, jingling around loose change in his jeans pocket. He looked like an Oriental James Dean.

"Bobbi," I told him, "is working a couple of evening shifts this week."

His mouth curved down — no smiles tonight — and with a nod of his head he said in a real quiet voice, "Come on out, okay?"

"Want me to fix you something cold to drink?"

"No, I'm not thirsty." He jumped off the step and onto the lawn, all shoulders and hunched-up jacket under the cricket-sounding night sky.

I grabbed my shoes and followed him out to the valley road. Then we walked almost the whole distance — two and a half miles — to Norton Crossings.

Nobody has talked to me so much in a year as Phil talked to me that night. He said it would have been his mother's birthday.

A huge tear, which he didn't bother to wipe away, slid down one side of his face. I saw it just as it reached his chin, before it rolled off onto his flipped-up collar.

I don't think my father has cried a single day since my mother died.

Phil's cigarette glowed under a flat white moon. A pelican flew over our heads, its neck stretched, its wings rustling like the sound my mother's evening dress used to make when she walked across the carpet from her closet to her makeup table. The bird landed, slapping around in a beam of light on the dark water, then bobbed along. When we turned around to go home again, it turned, too.

"I should have been with them" — Phil turned — "but I'd stopped going, and so he ignored me. He'd never beg — that wasn't his way." He stopped to squash his cigarette on the road.

I tried to think of how that might be, to have such religious parents. Mom was a kind of quiet Catholic, and all I know is that she prayed — she kept an amethyst crystal rosary wrapped in a lace-edged handkerchief in her top dresser drawer. Dad is an atheist. I've been to church maybe five times (one of those times to the funeral). While Mom was alive, Bobbi went more than any of us — to the only one in the village of Norton Crossings (popu-

16

lation seventy-five, including dogs), a United Church —
and that was because her friend Sally Towers, who's now
married and living in the city, wanted her to sing alto in
the church choir. Sally was the only other alto.

There's a Catholic church at the town of Crystal Lake,
fifteen miles down the valley, and even though we go there
for groceries and Friday night movies, we've never gone
there for religion.

"Maybe the dead can see us," I said, kicking a stone,
sending it bouncing crazily off into the roadside grasses.
"You know, for quite a while after she died I could feel
Mom's arms very tight around me just by wishing it." I
stretched my neck at the stars and named one for her —
Eugenie Augusta Fallows. I hoped she hadn't just disappeared. I often thought about the possibility that she
might still be somewhere, watching me.

"Do you believe in heaven, Phil? Or something? I don't
mean some fairy-tale fantasy with God sitting on a cloud.
But someplace real and peaceful — don't you think?"

"I don't have any beliefs," he said. "My parents aren't
anywhere now. They're finished. Gone."

He dug his hands into his pockets and walked away. He's
slim, but he's strong, and almost a head taller than Roberta. But in the weird light — turning his longish rumpled
hair, his jeans and jacket a smoky bluish gray — he looked
like he could disappear. Easy as a shadow. I'd be left alone
in the dark with the star and that spooky bird that seemed
to be watching me.

I ran to catch up. Only when I was right behind Phil did
he actually slow down. And when I started to walk beside
him again, he stopped and turned his back to me. He

17

hugged his arms to his chest and looked out over the moon-filled lake.

"You took off on me," I said, gasping for breath. "How would you like to be left alone in the night with a goddamn pelican?"

He said, turning, "I'm sorry."

"I thought we were taking this walk together, Phil."

"We are. Of course we are." He pulled me against his jacket. It smelled of tobacco and after-shave. He kissed the top of my head, and I didn't want to let him go. I kept holding on to him and squeezing my eyes shut tight. He was so warm, and I was starting to feel happy and calm. But he dropped his arms too soon and started walking again.

You can never hold anybody as long as you want. It's a rule that you won't find written anywhere, but it is one all the same.

As we walked home I wished that I could even just hold his hand. I guess it was a stupid little thing to wish.

"In a couple of hours," I said, "it'll be midnight. We'll walk until then, okay? Until her birthday is over?"

3 ⟶⟋

I 've just finished reading *Anne of Green Gables* for the seventh time, and I'm now wading through *Walden* by Henry David Thoreau. Dad's impressed but doesn't think I'll finish reading it. I've got news for him — if he's ever home long enough. Since Mom died, he's developed this habit of going around in an extremely large fog. He hasn't a clue, for instance, how much Bobbi and Phil and I have become kind of a summer family.

We might be at the kitchen table playing Monopoly and having cinnamon toast and hot cocoa or something domestic like that, and he'll walk through the door with this dazed expression, as if he's just coming up for air.

He'll make some remark to Phil, like, "Did they get back from the city with that shipment of blood?" just as if they were walking past each other on the wards at the infirmary.

Then he'll wander off aimlessly down the dark hallway, with Bobbi calling after him, "Did you have supper, Dad?"

Half the time he doesn't answer her. He simply hasn't heard.

Last winter it was just him and me. Well, more me than him. I'd get home after another cold dreary ride on the school bus (from Crystal Lake Collegiate Institute, a new improved "consolidated" high school where every teenager in the valley is now bused). Mrs. North would already be gone, and the place would be clean so it was like having a ghost for a housekeeper.

In the seven months between Roberta leaving for university and coming back, I saw Mrs. North exactly twice. The first time was around Thanksgiving, the second just before Christmas. Both times she had been held up cleaning the good silverware that nobody bothers with anymore. Before I'd even taken off my coat she'd grabbed her own and scurried past me out the door. It's not that she isn't kind. One time I found a loaf of homemade bread on the kitchen counter, and another time two plastic barrettes (which she must have figured I'd wear) on my pillow. I think, though, she's uncomfortable around death. She must think it's catching.

As soon as I'd get home from school I'd do my homework. And then, because there wasn't anything else to do, I'd cook something extravagant to add to the already gigantic pile of uneaten experiments in the fridge. Around six o'clock, when it was totally dark outside, the phone would ring. It would be Dad.

"Did you have a good day?" In the almost a year since Mom died, his voice has changed. It's tighter and softer and lower. He breathes in a tired way.

"Fine," I'd say. "How was yours?"

"Fine," he'd answer back. Then there would be the Pause. After that he would continue, his voice sounding farther away (did he hold the receiver between chin and shoulder, checking his watch?). "If you don't mind, I'll be staying here a little longer."

"I don't mind," I'd reply. Why did he bother to call every day and tell me the same thing?

"Good," he'd say. He was always relieved. "You're all right, then?"

"Yes. I'm fine."

"Well, then. I'll see you later."

"Yes. Good-bye."

Same scintillating conversation every day. I had better conversations with the cat. In fact, I had a better time with the cat. Humphrey Bogart. He and I would play cards on my bed after I'd eaten my dinner standing up in the kitchen.

Bogie is eight years old and his belly, from all my winter experimentation, skims his toes. He looks like a bulldog from behind but is actually a box-shaped Manx cat — a special breed from the Isle of Man. There are rumpies (no tail) and stumpies (a small stump). He is the former, and a black and tan tabby with bobcat-size paws and a big nose that's exactly the same shade as Pink Pearl erasers.

The night Mom died, Bogie lay on my hair on my pillow and chattered and purred, his warm breath against my ear, while I watched the trees outside the window make long finger shadows on my wall. He has always been a good friend to me.

We still play Fish on my white chenille bedspread. He settles down in front of me and watches as I fan out his

21

cards, then mine. "What have you got, there, Bogie? Two eights? Would you like mine? Here. No, I don't have another. Go fish for it. And I'll take all your queens, thank you very much." He's always making noises. You just have to say, "Hi, Bogie," and he'll squawk something back. Whatever it is he's trying to say, it always sounds interesting.

Most nights, during the winter, Dad would get home around nine o'clock. I'd hear the front door echo shut, his boots fall on the vestibule floor, the clink of a wire hanger. He'd then go into the kitchen, snap on the light, throw the mail on the counter, plug in the kettle for his tea, and pretty soon his feet would sound on the stairs. By that time, the card game over, I'd be reading. Bogie would have lost all interest in having a conversation, and I'd have stopped prodding him with my foot to get him to wake up and talk to me. He'd actually be snoring — little whistles and whines.

Dad would lean against the door frame holding his tea, watching me while I didn't look up from my book. He'd finally tiredly wipe his face with his freckled hand and ask what I was reading. Then I'd look up and tell him. He'd say, "Oh, he's a good author," or, "That was your mother's book. I've never read it," and sometimes, "I'm impressed. You'll study that one at university."

He'd slowly sip his tea. Between sips, I'd flip pages.

"You're okay?" he'd ask. Always the same question.

"Fine," I'd say. I miss Mom. I miss Roberta. Why do you come home so late? Why am I always alone in this big house? Don't you even care about me?

He'd nod his head, his eyes tired and empty. "That's good."

22

Mom was discharged from the infirmary as a patient when I was six and Bobbi was nine. For three years we hadn't been allowed to see her except through screens as Dad held us each by the hand, outside, under the branches of tall lichen-crusty oaks. On one of the second-story sleeping porches in the west wing, Mom would always appear — even on frosty winter days — bundled up under the arm of some nurse. "Wave to Mommy," Dad would say with a big smile. We'd all wave, and smile and smile. I didn't understand why Bobbi and I couldn't go to her. By my bed I kept a picture of her, which I kissed every night after prayers (I was still on reasonably friendly terms with God back then).

That photograph eventually seemed more real to me than Mom, waving to us from behind the screens.

I don't often go inside the infirmary (no one under the age of eighteen who isn't a patient is allowed on the wards). I haven't been there since one night last winter when it didn't seem as if Dad would actually make it home. Around two in the morning I got worried, hauled on my boots, pulled his old parka over my pajamas, and stumbled through about a dozen snowbanks to find him curled up asleep under a gray blanket on the maroon leather couch inside his dinky office. I was so angry that I didn't even wake him up. I just walked back out into the snow and left him there.

4 ⟿

I walk into our house carrying one of Mom's roses. It's six o'clock. Across the street Mrs. Coates is still on her knees on her lawn. With her bum in the air, she is fighting dandelions. Dr. Elsa McMorran has just trudged past her up the front walk to her house. The McMorrans' hi-fi, which only a minute ago blared Buddy Holly singing "Rave On," is now dead quiet. Their screened-in porch hides their living room. I'm almost positive, though, that it *is* her son, the boy we saw this afternoon at the beach, who's inside that house.

I drop the rose into the glass bowl on the kitchen table. I push up one of the four windows. Past the screen a robin flies up from the ravine and lands under the whirring lawn sprinkler.

Roberta, at the stove squashing a hamburger, says, "There isn't enough salt in your coleslaw."

She only wants me in *her* kitchen if, like today, she's running late.

"My coleslaw is perfect, Bobbi. And if you don't like the way I do things, then don't ask for my help."

"I only made a suggestion. You are *so* touchy."

I go into the living room. I push up the window behind the hi-fi. The McMorrans' house is directly across the street. Crouching down, I flip through Phil's pile of records. He's practically moved in, which is fine with me. I swear every record he owns is on the floor, propped up against the hi-fi cabinet.

I pull out "Drums on Fire!" flip side two onto the turntable, crank up the volume. A blast of horns, wild and jangled — Art Blakey and the Jazz Messengers. I'll bet that Toronto boy never heard anything like *this* before. If he could see me now, he'd think he's never seen anything like me, either.

I dance around the room like a beatnik, shaking my hair, snapping my fingers. (I'm in a dingy basement club. The room is filled with blue smoke. Everybody is cool and they're all wearing black and they all watch me jazz-dance.)

Out of the corner of my eye, I catch Phil coming through the front hall door. He's left it open so that he can turn and wave at Mrs. Coates. As usual, she's probably pretending not to see him so he won't think that she practically keeps a ledger on his comings and goings.

"Give her a wave for me, too," I say, breaking my jazz form with a pirouette. "She's such a lovely lovely woman."

25

He gives her an extra airy wave. He shakes his head. "She's not looking."

I arabesque past him and wave to her bum, singing softly, "Hello, Mrs. Coates, you nosy old bat." Then I close the door and leap gracefully back into the living room.

Today, Phil wears a cream-colored shirt and matching pants. He throws a thick medical text and a set of keys on the hall table. I'm back to jazz-dancing. He smiles, goes over to the hi-fi, turns down the sound. I grab his hands and make him spin me around the room. He indulges me, still smiling. His hands are cool; his forehead is sweaty. "How's the world treating you, sweet Georgia Brown?"

"Good," I say, smiling wildly.

"That's real cool." Then he pulls away and goes to find Bobbi.

They have a complicated relationship. Phil is outgoing one minute, moody the next, and he'd definitely like to make a play for her. Me, he treats like a kid sister. But her, he rarely touches.

Boys call Roberta a terrible tease. Normally she really fits the description. I can't figure out what she's feeling for Phil. She treats him less and less like every other boy she's ever known. Here's an interesting development: Bobbi, who's always hated to cook, has taken to making dinner every night for her "good friend" and me.

I can't help worrying that she's found a new way to lead somebody on. This would be no skin off my nose if it weren't for the fact that Phil is the most. Her other "beaus" have been too dumb to even mention — like Crawford, who wore nerdy glasses and could hardly ever get his eyes to move above her chin — which made him look as if he were always talking to the bumps under her angora sweaters. What a drip.

I go over to the hi-fi, lift the arm off the record. I fall onto the sofa, waiting for Phil. Dangle one foot over the back. Grab a cushion and balance it on my stomach.

Finally he comes back and sits down at the piano. He has fabulous hands — what Dad calls surgeon's hands. And he learned to play the way he does from some guy who grew up in New Orleans and lived in Toronto in the apartment above Phil and his brother. Quick as anything he's all over the keys with "It's Only a Paper Moon." I swing my legs off the sofa. He moves over for me to squeeze onto the piano bench beside him. Sort of nudges me with his shoulder.

This is the only part of the day I really look forward to.

Looking toward the kitchen, he serenades Roberta. She appears, all smiles and glowing attractively with grease and sweat. Her perfect sleeveless blouse is neatly tucked into cuffed white short shorts. Her dainty toenails are painted red to match her lipstick and fingernails.

Phil winks at her and hollers, " *'But it wouldn't be make believe, if you believed in me.'* "

"Dinner's ready, you nut." She swats the air over his head.

Laughing, he ducks his head, and then he takes off all over the keyboard again.

He's always happy when he's at the piano, jumping up and down the keys like a madman. He'd like to be a doctor in Montreal because, he tells me, it's the jazz capital of Canada. But more than likely he'll move back to Toronto where his brother has been a doctor for quite a while. He's

27

paying for Phil's education, and he runs the show. Phil jokes that George will likely pick out a suitable bride for him — a nice Chinese girl from a good family — and I don't think it's too far off from what'll actually happen. It'll serve Bobbi right.

In the kitchen, she has set out the coleslaw and a plate piled with enough hamburgers for six people.

"This looks good," says Phil as we sit down to eat. "What'd you guys do today?"

"Beach." Bobbi bites into her burger.

"How about tomorrow? Day off?"

"Two days together this week. You?"

"Tomorrow. Nothing after that until Tuesday."

They avoid each other's eyes. They eat like there's a famine in the land. In the morning Phil will show up at our back door for breakfast, and then he'll casually suggest we all go to the beach together, and Bobbi will act like it's the first time either one of them has thought of it. Then, once we get there, they'll fool around in the water and, after, lie on towels in the sun pretending they aren't close enough to touch. During all of this phony-baloney, I'll hang around like a fifth wheel while they both ignore me and I feel lonelier and lonelier.

The hamburgers are dry and gray. I shake a lot of ketchup onto mine. In the middle of the table the dark pink rose floats in the glass bowl. Red ants swim around it. Some have sunk, legs sprawled, to the bottom.

5 ⟿

Roberta and Phil laugh and splash around in the water, sending huge sprays up along the shore. They're faking it that they are just two buddies, horsing around. They won't shut up.

Bobbi yells, "Stop it!"

Phil's hoisted her, by her waist, right up out of the water, and he's laughing, threatening to throw her in. "Want to go for a swim now?"

"No!"

"Okay. I'll just pull you under."

"Phil, stop!"

But she doesn't mean it. Her hands are on his shoulders. She smiles down into his eyes.

Suddenly, he lets her drop. He's still holding on and now she's looking up at him. "Stop what?" he says with a low chuckle.

She giggles and weakly pushes him away. He gives her a

know-it-all look and shakes his finger at her. She splashes him. He splashes her back.

They're so hot for each other, I might as well not even be here.

Across the lake a summer cottage is being built — one hammer, then a second, banging away. These two hammers are annoyingly out of time. *Bangbang. Bangbang. Bang. Pause. Bang. Pausebang. Pausebangabang.*

It's a conspiracy to drive me bananas. You have to concentrate to read Thoreau's *Walden.* Dad gave me most of Mom's books because, he said, she considered me the serious reader in the family. There's this one line that I keep reading over and over again, "Take up a handful of the earth at your feet, and paint your house that color." I shade my eyes, look out on the lake.

Maybe what Thoreau is saying is, "Be honest and show your true colors." He could be talking about my own house, about my own family — who walk around acting as if everything's perfectly fine when everything's actually quite hopeless. I should cut out that line and tape it to Bobbi's mirror.

Out in the lake something moves. I keep watching. Clear and shiny, long arms and a head — a swimmer, heading straight for shore, who's fast and doesn't miss a beat.

Phil shakes water from his hair, pushes it back from his forehead. Bobbi's sopping hair clings like red-blond flames down her shoulders. They both turn, surprised, as Elsa McMorran's son shoots past them, thrashing up foam. His arms and head are caught in the most amazing arc of water.

30

He's about twenty feet from shore. Suddenly his arms stop pumping. He sinks. Gasping for breath he gets to his feet. He sheds pounds of water and staggers past me.

I look down. *Walden* has become a pond. I hold it up, and that only makes matters worse. Some of the water flows away. Most of it seeps into the pages.

He's found a toehold in the granite table rock under the oak tree and has hauled himself up. Now he sprawls, panting, on his back. Rolling his head to the side, he coughs, settles his arms against the heat, and closes his eyes. His swimming trunks trickle thin streams of water down the side of the rock.

Mom's book is ruined. Her name, written in dark blue fountain pen ink, runs down the front page in blue tears. I dab at it with the corner of my towel. It smears even more. Her name is so faint now, I can hardly read it.

Water hits my spine. I look up. It's Bobbi, dripping, her back to the sun. She frowns down at me.

"Disgusting." She wrinkles her perfect nose. "You're making that towel filthy."

"Bobbi, drop dead and roll your measly corpse down an anthill."

She whips the towel — raining black shale — out of my hands.

Phil sits on the dock calmly lighting a cigarette as if he hasn't noticed this display.

Bobbi walks away from me, her hips swaying for his benefit as he finally looks up. He smiles, pretending not to be moved by her little performance, and quickly looks away.

I crack open the book at the middle and leave it in the

direct sun. But even if it dries out, it'll never be the same again.

The boy from Toronto, his skin all beaded with water and stretched tight below his rib cage, relaxes on the rock.

I stand up. In a clear, well-modulated voice I say, "Thanks for ruining my book, jerk." He doesn't move. He hasn't heard. It's as though he doesn't have a care in the world. His navel shows just above the waistband of his blue swimming trunks. One knee is bent; one arm dangles down the side of the rock.

"Hello? I said thank you for ruining my book — are you deaf?"

He lifts his head, startled — his hazel eyes are flecked with gold, like his hair. He sits up. Then he slides down the rock. His feet hit the beach. Slowly, he walks over and stands beside me. I glance down at the book. He strokes his chin with a large tanned hand and looks off down the beach at nothing in particular. The other hand he places on his hip. He then looks straight into my eyes and says, "I didn't do that."

"You sure as hell did. And you'd just better buy me a new one."

He makes an inspection of the book — lifts it with a tanned toe, his arms folded across his bare chest. He clenches his teeth. Works his jaw muscles. "That's pretty stupid to leave it out in the sun like that, don't you think?"

I say, incredulously, "It's completely soaked. My God, it's beyond repair." I snatch up *Walden*. "You are — are just — an utter idiot!"

He stands back looking alarmed, alert, and *amused!*

I stomp through the sand and shale over to Roberta.

32

She is using my towel as a pillow. "I'm going to walk home, and I need this," I say, whipping it out from under her.

Phil, now lying on his back, opens one eye as Bobbi's head makes a satisfying thunking sound on the wooden dock. With an exasperated sigh, he turns his head away. Bobbi sits straight up. "Are you crazy — what's wrong with you?"

"I am not crazy, Roberta. I am mad," I say, knotting the soggy towel around my waist. "And I'm sure you and Phil and — and What's-His-Name over there will have a perfectly lovely time without me. Good-bye."

6 ⟋⊚⟍

P eter Stafford, the only boy I've ever really gone
out with, lived on a farm three miles outside
Crystal Lake. I met him on my first day at the Collegiate,
just two weeks after Mom died.

I'd come on the bus — I knew a few of the other stu-
dents, but as we got closer to Crystal Lake the kids who got
on were mostly total strangers. By grade ten quite a number had failed a grade or two, dropped out, and were
working, pregnant, married, or all three.

I walked into this huge high school, with hundreds of
yelling people all trying to find their homerooms. A
woman in a brown tweed suit and brown oxfords and thick
brown stockings told me to go down the hall, down the
stairs, outside to the boardwalk, and out across the grass to
the grade ten hut.

It was insane. I'd never seen so many people in one place
in my life, and you could tell the town girls because they

all walked together in clusters, whispering. They gave me their *Oh gawwwd — who's sheeee?* stares. I immediately hated them, their sack dresses and their poodle haircuts.

I found the right hut, which turned out to be one of four lined up at the back of the school to take care of the new overflow. I took an empty seat at the back really close to the door.

"This is my desk," said some idiot, slamming his books down on top of mine just as I was going to sit.

"Geez, Arnold," said a boy with bright green eyes and brown hair. He stood beside his own desk, halfway across the room. "C'mere," he said to me, with a nod of his head.

I grabbed up my books, held them tight against my chest, and froze.

He laughed. "I don't bite — honest."

"Don't count on it — think fast, Stafford," cackled the idiot, hucking an eraser at him.

So I went and sat at the empty desk in front of Peter Stafford.

And then the stupidest thing happened. He asked me out on a date, and I said yes. He and his brother, Garry, picked me up in their father's red Chevy truck and then drove us all the way back to Crystal Lake, where we were dropped off to see *Rebel Without a Cause* at the Roxy. In the darkened theater Peter shyly reached for my hand, and he held it all through the movie. His hand was big and a bit rough and callused, but he held mine inside, gently, almost nervously — as if he were scared it would break — as we watched the silver screen. That was on a Friday night. He said he'd call on Saturday. He didn't. Not on Sunday either.

I got back to school on Monday, and he wasn't there. I figured maybe he was sick or had to work. It isn't unusual for farm boys to take off a few days from school at harvest-time so they can help out at home. Teachers don't say much. This is a farming community.

Some girl came up to me in French class. She said, "You knew Peter Stafford, didn't you?"

"Knew?" I said stupidly.

"He got killed this weekend," she said. "A grain truck backed over him."

Half the town kids and all the farm kids from right around Crystal Lake went to Peter Stafford's funeral. Some people went, I think, because they were curious. But most went because they really liked him.

I didn't go. I kept thinking about his strong gentle hands and his plaid snap-button shirt and the smell of the Dentyne gum he chewed that night he came to pick me up and, after meeting Dad, as we were leaving, how he looked around the kitchen with a big friendly smile and asked, "Your mom away somewhere?"

After that I didn't talk much to people, even if they seemed friendly. I just stuck to myself. I sat in the same desk in the grade ten hut. And I didn't turn around. I pretended he was still there.

7

W hen Roberta left for her shift in the infirmary, early this morning, she prodded at me the way she would a dead animal with a stick.

"Get the dishes done and clean up this house. I've just discovered jam on the new sofa covers that I spent two whole weeks sewing, and it won't come off. I am sick and tired of doing everything myself and then having it slopped on. I have absolutely had it with you."

She paused in her Witch Queen Routine.

"Oh, dry up," I said, rolling over, groggy with sleep.

"When Mrs. North comes back, in the fall, you can make all the mess you want. Until then I will not be your servant."

"Neither is she," I said — yawning just to bug her. "Mrs. North is actually a figment of everybody's imagination. Dad's paying a ghost."

She tugged on the metal rings on the dark green blinds,

which then flapped to the tops of my windows. The morning sun, already hot, flooded in and stabbed my eyes.

"Roberta, you are such a pain. Find a bridge, okay?"

She ranted on: "Know what your problem is?"

"Oh, please, I really want to know."

"You are afraid of growing up and accepting responsibility."

"Spare me the details."

"And you are so lazy that it's unbelievable. It's practically pathological. You need medical help."

I thrashed around on my bed as if I'd just finally flipped out. That really got her going. I had to put my pillow over my face to drown her out.

When she finally slammed out of the house the walls shook — she is so well adjusted and mature.

I got up and sat on the edge of my bed for a while. I'm a chronic insomniac, and it had been a bad night. I tried to think of any reason why I might want to get up. It's a little game I play. I poke away at my life in the morning, trying to find something good. Anything will do — playing another card game with Bogie, eating anything from the fridge that doesn't remind me of breakfast, reading a book I want to finish reading.

I got off the bed and looked out the windows. My corner bedroom has windows overlooking the backyard and ravine on one side, and right below on the other is the rose garden. I slapped, barefoot, out into the hallway and went across to my parents' room.

Their windows overlook the street. Across it, at eye level, is an umbrella-shaped elm that shades the second story of Elsa McMorran's house. The branches lightly swayed, making the sun and shadows bounce up and down in splotches on the bedroom windows.

The two other houses on this sawed-off street are occupied by Mr. (Arthur) and Mrs. (Nosy) Coates — he's the sanatorium's engineer — and also by Donina Stang, the dietitian whose husband goes away for weeks at a time to do whatever geologists do.

Donina likes me to call her by her first name. She wears her black hair bouncy and kind of curled under and a bit over her eyes, like Marilyn Monroe in *Some Like It Hot*, and one day when I was reading up on our flat roof, she stood up on hers — right next to Dr. McMorran's. I hadn't noticed her there before. She smiled and waved, which was a bit of a shock because she sunbathes in the nude. She isn't bothered by what anybody says about her. And they say plenty. She once gave me a pair of Thai silver and black dangly earrings because she was wearing them at the time I admired them. She grew up all over the world. She's half British, half East Indian, speaks five languages, is definitely eccentric, and loves movies — any movie, old or new — like me.

It's now close to noon. I've hidden behind the living room curtains to facilitate this spy job. Dr. M. will have left early, of course — and Brainless Adonis can't stay in there forever. Sooner or later, in this heat, he's going to have to come out and go for another swim.

Yesterday, after ruining my mother's book, he dogged my footsteps all the way home. Twice, he whistled long and low at me. (I don't know — maybe he thought I'd faint from uncontrollable urges and fall back into his arms.)

When I turned up our street, so did he. As I ducked my

39

head between the two monstrous fir trees that partially shade our front yard, he drawled, "Nice legs." I heard him clomp up his front porch steps.

I do have nice legs. So charming of him to notice.

Their windows are all closed. What sort of person leaves all the windows closed on such a hot day? For the past half hour I've been concentrating on his front door, willing it to open.

This morning, just because I felt like it, I "borrowed" Roberta's sexy new bathing suit, and I'm wearing it under my green shorts and sleeveless pink blouse. I've pulled back my hair into a high, tight ponytail.

I turn from the window to examine my hair in the front hall mirror. I look like Carmen Miranda. All I need is a hat with bananas. Hotcha, hotcha, baby. I'm such a geek. Should I wear my hair down? Maybe I should just wear a bag on my head. Maybe I should go and eat something.

In the kitchen I make myself half a bologna and lettuce sandwich. I toss the knife into the sink. It pings off the side of a cereal bowl and clatters into last night's dishes and this morning's floating Rice Krispies. I squeak over the hardwood floors, down the hall, over to the windows.

He's wearing blue jeans with a loose blue shirt, and he's almost reached the lake road!

I take the hall stairs two at a time. In the bathroom I grab the Listerine bottle. Take a swig, slosh it all around my teeth, spit it all at once into the sink.

As I lift my arms to smooth my eyebrows I'm shocked to see about two weeks' worth of stubble on my armpits. I dig out Dad's safety razor, quickly lather up with soap, and nick myself. Blood runs onto my sleeveless shirt. I whip it

40

off, throw it into the laundry basket by the tub, and, holding a towel to my armpit, dash to his closet. Raking through suits and pants, I come across a freshly ironed white dress shirt. I pull it on and am tying the knot at my waist as I hit the first stair landing. Rolling up the sleeves, I stumble into my sneakers in the front hall. Out the door.

The tires on my bike have been flat since the last week in April. I take Roberta's and make for the valley road. Clattering on south, I see his shirt far up ahead — billowing up in the breeze like a hot air balloon. I bend over the handlebars and pedal hard.

When I finally look up, I see that I'm gaining on him. Taking long strides, he sort of shoulders and struts along.

All at once he hears me and turns around, startled. He jumps right back out of my way. Almost falls over. The shirt, completely undone, flaps away from his body. His pointed nipples are small and brown.

I brake the bike, get off, and casually remove Roberta's sunglasses. My hand is trembling. My legs are like rubber. I am now going to demand that he pay me two dollars and seventy-five cents, which is what my mother paid for *Walden* five years ago (the price is still penciled in on the front page, beside her water-streaked name).

But he stands there in the ditch, with a stunned expression like he's just been attacked by a crazy person. That really finishes me, that look. I walk the bike away in a hurry.

Grasses swish around his legs as he comes out of the ditch and quickly follows me.

"There's blood on your shirt," he calls.

"It's my father's shirt," I say, not looking back. "He cut himself shaving."

"On his arm?"

"He's very careless."

"He must be."

I stop and turn. Little stones grind under his feet, and he trudges right up and stares into my eyes. I feel as if I am being examined under a very strong light. I drop my eyes to his chest. Wrong place to look. Quickly, I focus on the handlebars of my bike and push on ahead.

"I'm Kieran McMorran," he says, right in step beside me. "And I've just moved from Toronto to be with my mom for a while. Or possibly forever. I hate it here. And," he adds, "I like your hair better down than up."

"Sidonie Fallows," I barely whisper. I want to pull the elastic out of my hair, but that would be too obvious.

He bends his head, "What's that, again?"

"My name is Sidonie. It's French. Sid-on-ee," I say, turning up my face to look at him again. The top of my head just reaches his shoulder.

"Sidonie." He's looking down at my mouth. His full rounded lips are hypnotizing.

Something like a light after-shave, or maybe it's his shampoo, gets mixed up with the west wind off the lake. I feel extreme misery and extreme something else — all at the same time. I can't speak.

"Do you always run people down?" he asks with a small teasing smile. His eyes don't once flicker away from my face.

He can see everything I'm feeling. I'm worried that my legs won't hold me up. "I was on my way somewhere," I lie,

42

and blush. I point my nose down the road and move along a little faster.

He says, so close I can feel the heat from his body, "Yesterday I was in a pretty bad mood. Swear to God, though, I didn't notice your book."

I move faster still. "My mother paid for it. It was her book."

"Well, then, I'll pay her for it."

I'm practically running. He is, too. We're pounding along, breathless. He suddenly grabs the handlebars. The bike bangs against my legs. My feet skid along on the slippery gravel, and he brings me, the bike, and himself to a full stop.

"I have to go," I say, forcing myself to look at him.

"Why?" he says, and now he's grinning as though this is all a big joke.

"I just have to. That's all. So please just let me go."

Right away he lifts his hands. Holds them up as if the metal has burned his skin. He stands back and gives me another huge grin.

"My mother is dead," I say, and I don't wait around to see his smile fade. I wheel the bike around, get on, and push off home.

8 ⟋⊙⟍

There's this nightmare that tends to creep into my dreams when I've finally fallen asleep after having a really crappy day.

Roberta and I are at a summer fair at the town of Crystal Lake. We're stopped on a Ferris wheel, high up where oceans of yellow waving wheat roll away for miles. Our feet poke at mountain-size clouds. It's a perfect clear-aired summer day. Roberta and I wiggle our toes and swing back and forth in a little August breeze. We know we have to get home to Mom.

"There's no rush," says Roberta, stretching her arms, waving them around in the blue sky. "Isn't this the most beautiful day?"

I agree with her. But the Ferris wheel seems stuck in one spot forever. We're at the very top. A field, off to one side, looks like a bed. I'm worried that I'll see Mom's face. That

I'll have to watch her die. I lean over to tell Roberta. Except it isn't Roberta who's sitting beside me.

It's Mom — smiling at me, smelling of roses, her dark hair in a French roll. She pulls out the pins, and the wind catches it, blowing it out behind her like an immense Chinese fan.

"I'm so tired, Sidonie," she whispers. "Won't you brush it for me?"

I brush her hair. I brush it and brush it and brush it and brush it. It crackles like a thunderstorm. The wind picks up, and we start to rock. My arms are aching, but I have to keep brushing or she'll die. I have to take care of her. The sky gets as dark as night, except it's still day. The wind smells reedy, like the lake, and I can't see Mom anymore and I can't find her in the dark. I feel as if I'm going to drown. Then I *am* drowning, turning over and over in the deep night-filled water, slowly being crushed by the weight of the lake.

It's always at this point that I wake up. I'm dizzy. I'm still spinning. Yet my whole body feels pushed into the bed. I wait for the feeling to pass.

Then what I see, what I remember, is the ambulance outside our house. That hot August day, Roberta and I *had* gone to the Crystal Lake Fair. And when we got back, driving slowly into the driveway, she said, "Oh, my God, what's happened?" even though we both knew, right away. Little stones pinged under the tires, and the ambulance roof towered above our car window. Dad was there to meet us. He looked so stern and pale. He wanted to do everything properly. To tell us exactly how it had happened.

I ran down into the ravine. I didn't want his stupid facts. I only wanted someone to hold me. I sat on some moss, still holding the candy apple I'd been keeping until I got home. I rolled it over and over in my hands. I could hardly feel it move as I watched the gooey candy redden my skin. The thin stick just kept whirling madly back and forth until a slow kind of painful heat came prickling up my body. Then I was sweating, and then I was cold, and then I was hot again.

In the little creek, the water gurgled over the rocks the way it had done for probably hundreds of summers. I tossed the apple away and bent my face over the water. I didn't want to think about next summer. How dare there be one, or one after that, or one after that without my mother? I splashed my face with the water. It wasn't cold, and it didn't help. I didn't even get the chance to tell her good-bye.

9 ⟶◎⟶

E xcept for three totally necessary trips to the bathroom, I've been stuck in my room since one
o'clock yesterday afternoon, when I pedaled hard all the
way back to my house, wheeled off the sidewalk between
the two fir trees, dropped Bobbi's bike on the lawn, raced
up the steps to the front door (I gave it only a slight push
but it banged open anyway), caught the top part of my
sneaker on the doorsill, and tripped. My ankle went one
way, my body the other. I felt a piercing pain as if someone
had just taken a saw and hacked through my bones. In no
time at all, my whole foot started to swell.

I took two aspirin, a jug of orange juice, and a box of
crackers up to my room, shut Bogie in with me, and pulled
a stack of *Modern Screen* and *Life* and *Mad* magazines out
from under my bed. Then I stayed flat on my back all
afternoon.

Around five o'clock Bobbi and Phil came home. I

listened for Phil to go to the piano — something to take my mind off the pain. Instead, I heard him coming up the stairs (his style is quiet as a panther, two at a time — only the hardwood creaks).

He paused by my door. "Sidonie?"

I didn't answer him.

"I know you're in there — anything the matter?"

I thought about this, and I said, "Nothing."

He paused by the door — I could practically hear him breathing — and then he asked, "What's up?"

"Go away," I said, rattling the April issue of *Life* that has Marilyn Monroe on the cover.

After a few seconds he muttered, "You're too old to behave like this." Then he went away.

A couple of minutes later, Roberta came up and banged on my door. I told her to drop dead and go to hell.

Dad rapped on my bedroom door around ten o'clock. He came into the room and stood in a shaft of light while I lay with my eyes half closed so I could still more or less see him.

He said, "Your sister wants to know what's wrong with you."

I pulled the covers over my face and said, miserably, "There's nothing wrong with me. I'm perfectly fine."

He sighed heavily and went away, closing the door behind him.

Bogie abandoned me around midnight by prying open the door with his paws and escaping.

This morning I woke up feeling suffocated and sick. I whipped back the covers on my bed. My ankle is a seething red and is really rigid. It has swollen to the size of a small balloon.

It's pretty depressing, but I have to admit that this isn't just going to go away. I have to try to make it over to see Dad at the infirmary.

I stumble out of bed, jump around on one foot, and clutch at various walls. In the bathroom, I ease down onto the little white vanity chair that's by the sink. I pull on panties, a pair of white shorts, and Bobbi's strapless bra and her navy sleeveless blouse (both found dangling out of the laundry hamper). Then I brush my teeth and run a wet comb through my hair.

Out to the hall again, I make it over to the banister. Down to the first landing. Down to the collection of shoes in the front hall. I'm feeling so tired and sore I want to collapse and have vultures just sweep down and take me away. Can't put a shoe on my bad foot — the Cantaloupe. Decide to go barefoot. Hop out of the house to the top of the front steps. I cling to the railing.

I take one step and suddenly lose my balance. I keel right over and meet up with cement.

I'm lying here, my elbow's bleeding and I don't know what else. I seem to hurt all over. And now, who should I see — and he's practically running across the street — the jerk. Himself.

I sit up and burst into tears. I have to pretend that I'm actually laughing. He's coming right up to stand right over me.

I turn up my face to meet his. In it there isn't so much as a smirky smile, or anything else like I thought there would be. He's just looking down at my foot like any normal person seeing somebody in pain. "I was out on my porch, and I saw you fall," he says. "You fell real hard. I could almost hear your bones crack."

"Yeah, well, I did something to my ankle," I say, angrily rubbing my elbow over and over.

He sinks down beside me, resting on his heels in his bathing trunks, whistling softly. "You murdered it," he says seriously.

The short-sleeved shirt he wears over the trunks flutters around in the little wind that's easing through the branches of the fir trees. I can't help noticing how good he looks. A dark brown freckle floats like the tiniest island in the middle of his earlobe.

"Don't try to stand anymore," he says, and crinkles up his forehead.

"Okay," I say, wiping my nose with the back of my hand.

Quite suddenly, he slides over in front of me. He looks at my ankle as if it's the only thing that exists in the world. Then he looks up, and he's suddenly businesslike. "I'm a doctor's son," he says, as if he's been caught in a moment that's too private for anyone to see. "Actually," he continues, "*both* my parents are doctors. So I know something about injuries. Ever hurt your ankle before?" He reaches down and begins to stroke it with his big hands, his long fingers.

"Goddamn, goddamn, goddamn," I say, hanging my head, rocking back and forth.

"What's the matter?" He quickly pulls his hands away.

50

"I don't know," I whisper. But I do know. I'm all at once remembering Peter Stafford's hands and Mom's hands and I can't handle this. I feel suffocated; it's like there are ghosts all around me.

He leans right over so he can see up into my face.

"Please don't," I whisper.

"I broke my toe last summer," he says quickly, "and believe it or not, the pain got so bad that if a hatchet had been handy I'd probably have cut the frigging thing off." He sits back, clutching his knees. "We're at our cottage at Rice Lake, and Dad decides to pour me this massive glass of scotch — wants me to chugalug."

"Did you?" I wipe my face on the collar of Bobbi's blouse.

He looks at me again and says, "He was pretty damn hammered at the time. I hate scotch. He says it's a *man's* drink. I didn't think he'd notice, so I went into the can, spat it out, then puked, and then I did what I always do when all hell breaks loose. Lay on my bed with a pillow over my face and yelled."

"You do that?"

"Sounds pretty weird, doesn't it," he says, frowning.

"People do weird stuff when they're upset. I do all the time, as you can probably tell."

"Yeah?" He smiles at me. His *real* smile is wonderful. His face crumples up with a sweet kind of sudden release.

I smile back.

"You should give it a try sometime," he mumbles, with a sort of bearish swiping pat at my shoulder. "All the stale air under the pillow really calms a person down. Do you have a wagon?"

"A wagon?"

"A little kid's wagon. Mine's rusting under the porch at my house. My house in Toronto." He isn't looking at my ankle anymore. He's looking at my mouth.

I like the wet smell of his hair, the hot summery smell of his skin. I say, "It's in the shed in our backyard, I think. Behind a crib. It's yellow. The crib is yellow. The wagon is red. Of course."

"Right. Red." He smiles, raises his eyebrows, and rubs the back of his neck. "Behind the yellow crib." He stands. White sand and little bits of black shale cling to his bare tanned feet. I'll bet he spends half his life in the water. "Your foot," he proclaims, "could be broken. But then again, it might not be."

He goes around the roses side of the house. On the edge of our property, the peeling white shed backs onto woodlands that crowd right down the ravine to the creek.

I get a memory flash of the last time I used the wagon — about seven years ago — of making mud cakes and then popping them out of muffin tins into two neat rows along the bottom; of decorating them with leaves and then rushing inside the house to run my hands under the hot water tap because it was the middle of October and they were stinging with cold. It was Roberta who yelled at me about the muddy sink because that was the year — at the age of twelve — that she took over the after-school chore of making dinner for everybody.

In a little while, the wagon comes creakety-creaking through the grass. Kieran circles in behind me, dropping

52

the handle, then eases his hands under my armpits and half lifts, half pulls me backward on my good foot up over the side. He stands back, folding and unfolding his arms, watching as I try to arrange myself on the caked mud and dusty bronze oak leaves that cling inside the wagon.

10 ⟳

One leg is scrunched under me. The mangled foot hangs over the side, and I tighten my body against the bumping and jarring as Kieran tips the wagon up onto the hot white sidewalk.

"You're okay?" he asks.

"I'm fine," I say, and we start to roll again. There's no breeze except when we move.

The wagon bumps over the cracks, down the sidewalk, along the ivy-covered stone walls of the infirmary, past windowed offices, clacking typewriters, flower beds, and sleeping figures in beds on the second-story sleeping porches.

A little way back from the entrance, Kieran wheels the wagon under the shadowy green branches of a big oak. "Good place. Lots of shade," he says, coming back and hunkering down.

I'm still holding fast to the rusty metal sides as he's

leaning in. "Okay, now, arms around my neck," he says. And he puts his arms around me in a matter-of-fact way. But he's trembling slightly. I can feel it in his muscles. All at once I can tell that he likes me. It's his nervousness — like Peter Stafford when he held my hand at the movie theater. I feel tender and thrilled all at the same time.

"Oh," I say faintly, and, "sorry," jabbing him with my elbow as he stands up, holding me.

I hug my arms around his neck. Light sweat beads up over his full top lip. His cheek is smooth with little splotches of reddish pink showing under his tan. He smiles. I smile. He drops his eyes to my shoulder and I find a place past his ear, and my heart thuds into my throat.

The infirmary doors clatter open. "Hurry," says a voice.

I pull my face away. His arms loosen. I slide down his body. He hoists me up again.

Dr. McMorran has a round face and hair that's half gray and half brown and dark circles like bruises under her eyes. She's holding back one of the doors. "Don't drop her," she says in her slightly European accent.

"Cripes, it's my mother," Kieran whispers. His hot breath tickles my ear.

"I know," I say.

"Look at that ankle." Dr. McMorran lurches away from the heavy doors. They clatter behind her. She has cat's-eye glasses that hang around her neck from one of those pearly chains that everybody over fifty wears, and she's trying to untangle them as if she wants to examine me.

Red-faced, Kieran circles past her and says, "Mom, could you please get the doors?"

"Hello, Dr. McMorran." I smile over Kieran's shoulder

in an extremely friendly way. My ankle feels like it's full of little daggers. I want her to evaporate.

On the two other occasions that I saw Dr. McMorran, she didn't once crack a smile. I don't think she's unsociable, just unhappy. Her hand drops from her glasses. Her eyes dart from Kieran to me. "I'm glad you two have met," she says, all seriousness, to his back. She follows us, talking rapidly. "He says this place is lonely. I tell him, look who's right across the street." She zips around in front of him. "You're taking her to see her father?"

"Yes."

"Her foot looks bad."

"Yes," Kieran replies.

"Do you know where his office is?"

"I'll handle it, Mom."

"Of course. Of course."

He looks at me, sighs. "The world's biggest worrier."

I'm amazed to see Dr. McMorran smile. She's really quite a pretty lady. She lowers her head, pats his shoulder.

In a kind of Bogart lisp, he says, "Open the frigging door, sweetheart."

"That will be enough, son," she says, quickly raising her head and her eyebrows.

"She's got a great sense of humor" — he chuckles — "but you have to get her revved up first."

Dr. McMorran holds open the door, shooing us along. But you can tell that she's actually enjoying all of this. She's embarrassed but is still wearing a trace of a smile.

He pushes past. He doesn't notice when we hit my foot on the edge of the other door. I gasp in pain and then start to giggle, and then I can't stop.

56

An old man with a cane dozes like a statue in the waiting area. He doesn't wake up.

Kieran starts laughing until his whole body shakes. He's weakly staggering around with me in his arms. The old man's eyes flicker open. He smiles sweetly at us, and Dr. McMorran says, "I made a tuna fish casserole for supper. Are you listening?" (She's desperate to change the subject.) "The casserole is in the refrigerator. Put it in the oven at five o'clock. Three hundred fifty degrees. With cornflakes. Kieran, you are being rude."

Everything is hilarious. "Sorry, Mom," he snorts. "Breakfast cereal on the casserole."

"Hurry up, for heaven's sake," she says, marching off.

Her heavily starched coat rumbles, her rubber-soled shoes squeak, as she hurries down the echoey hospital-smelling corridor to the patient wards.

Dad is standing tall outside his office. A stooped-over patient is just leaving. She shuffles down the corridor in her pink furry slippers, arguing with herself, clutching and pulling at the top of her cotton dressing gown. Her dyed red hair is greasy but neatly combed into a little ball with sticking-out black bobby pins.

Dad isn't glad to see me, or my foot. He comes away from the door and slaps down the hair at the back of his head as we crowd past him into the small room. Kieran sets me down on the examining table.

"What happened to you?" Dad bends over my ankle, disapproving, as if I am to blame for the mess it's in.

I try holding my breath to calm down.

"It really hurts her, sir," says Kieran seriously. "I think it's broken."

Dad lightly presses the swollen red skin around my ankle bone and asks again, "How did you do this?"

"I fell," I say, bursting out giggling.

He sighs. Stands back. "You're hysterical. Are you able to move it?"

"Of course. I ran all the way." My foot has gone into a kind of spasm. It looks so hilarious, I'm practically falling off the table.

All flushed, arms held rigidly at his sides, Kieran says, "You'll probably need to take X rays."

Dad adjusts his glasses with two fingers. "I'm aware of that."

It doesn't feel good, this laugh. Everything starts to reel. "Dad," I say, "I think I'm going to be sick."

He grabs up a kidney basin and sticks it under my chin. Sweat burns, then chills my face. The silver metal is icy, and I hold my mouth over it and start to heave. The room seems to flip upside down. Dad pulls back my hair and patiently waits for me to finish vomiting.

When I finally look up, Kieran is gone.

11 ⟿

Roberta is being very nice to me. This is a tactic she uses only when she's desperate. I know exactly how she thinks. For this entire past week, building up in her mind is the thought that I have hurt myself on purpose so I can sprawl on the sofa for days on end, just to read by the hi-fi and listen to Art Blakey and Dave Brubeck and Little Richard and the Kingston Trio's "Hungry i" album and generally drive her crazy with my moods.

Across the street only one thing has happened to let me know that someone's clued in to the fact that I haven't died or anything. Yesterday, right after I played "Drums on Fire!" the McMorrans' hi-fi blasted all over the place with "Night in Tunisia." This means that Kieran McMorran is also a fan of Art Blakey and the Jazz Messengers. Worse luck for Art Blakey.

The X rays didn't reveal any broken bones. Dad thought

I might have torn a ligament and said it would likely take a week or so to start to heal, and it has.

At the infirmary he wrapped up my foot, put me on painkillers, and ordered one of the nurses to make up a bed for me in the high-ceilinged one-bed room they call sick bay.

I stayed there during the afternoon for observation (nobody came to observe me, not even Dad — unless it was while I was asleep). Finally, at six o'clock, who should appear around the doorway, grinning like crazy and dangling a pair of crutches, but Phil. "Your transportation, dollface," he said. "Let's vamoose."

Phil, who doesn't disappear even when people behave badly or injure themselves or *vomit*, owns six red hotels. This is our second game of Monopoly. He is the land baron of Boardwalk and Park Place.

I am chewing on a rope of licorice that I found in the drawer of the end table, and I refuse to leave Jail. He keeps offering to lend me money.

"C'mon, it's Saturday night," Roberta says, whisking away the Monopoly board. "Let's all take the car and go to the dance pavilion at Crystal Lake. I want to get dressed up. Wouldn't you like to go dancing, Phil?"

Yes. Yes. Yes. I've got her number. She feels guilty about last night when she and Phil went to the Friday movie at Crystal Lake (*The Defiant Ones* with Tony Curtis and Sidney Poitier, which I really wanted to see). Instead of letting me tag along like I usually do, they left me to rot in front of the boob tube. Now she's decided to make it up to me.

"I'm not exactly up to dancing, Bobbi, in case you

60

haven't noticed," I say, even though I'm planning to burn the crutches soon.

"Yes. But it would certainly do you good to get out," she says, pushing back her hair, sitting down on the edge of the sofa right by my foot.

"And how was your movie last night?"

"Oh. That." She twiddles with her pearl ring. "It was in black and white. I know you like Technicolor."

I can tell by the look on her face that it was a terrific movie and that it really impressed her. "I *know* it's in black and white. I've seen *photos* of it, Roberta. So why don't you just go to your dance and forget about me. I'm not in the mood."

She says quietly, looking over at Phil, "You don't have to dance, Sidonie."

"Oh, terrific. I'll sit there like a stone and watch you guys waltz around. That'd be just great."

"There will be other people there," says Phil, flicking on the TV. He perches on the edge of the piano seat to adjust the rolling picture and adds, "You need to be around people your own age."

"Thanks a big fat lot." I flop flat against the pillows, turning to punch one into shape. "If you can't stand being around me, then go. Who the hell is stopping you."

"We're not going without you," Roberta says sweetly, looking over at Phil again for moral support.

"You spend far too much time by yourself." Phil's back is turned in the way of cats when they pretend to be uninterested but are actually ready to perk up their ears at the teeniest sound.

Roberta, a woman used to getting her own way, runs

upstairs. Minutes later she's back in a full-skirted white dress, red cinch belt, red slip-ons, and daisy clip-on earrings. She tosses me her new formfitting black Bermuda shorts (which she knows I've been dying to get my hands on), my own red stretch strapless top, and her sheer white blouse (when I wanted to wear it last month, she told me, "Tough toenails").

"You must really want to go to this dance," I say, rolling over onto my good foot.

"You have no idea," says Roberta, glaring at me, "how hard it is to be nice to someone who is *always always always* in such a crappy mood."

"You needn't swear," I say lightly.

She walks behind me, breathing fire down my back, as I crutch up the hall stairs to the bathroom.

Our car is brand new — a 1959 Ford Fairlane 500, a two-door, with fins, red and white, whitewall tires. It has a push-button radio, dual headlights, and a Cruiseomatic transmission. It was Roberta, of course, who helped Dad pick it out. The red is the same shade as her lipstick, which, I figure, was part of the attraction. She gets to drive it most of the time, but whenever she and Phil go anywhere, she hands him the keys.

Rising over the valley, a pale harvest moon, all peaches and cream, is huge and misty as we set out. The silky wind off the lake is cool. Phil and Roberta are in the front seat and I'm in the back. Roberta pulls in her arm, leans over, and pushes up and down the radio dial until she gets to Jerry Keller singing "Here Comes Summer."

Roberta pulls out a cigarette. Phil is quick to give her a light. She puts out her hand to hold it steady, and her fingers stay on his a little longer than they need to. I think I saw Lauren Bacall do that to Humphrey Bogart in *Key Largo*. Phil's eyes glaze over. He clicks down the lid, leans back on the seat to get the lighter back into his pocket.

Roberta's head suddenly swivels around as she looks back down the road. Laying her thin freckled arm along the top of the seat, she says to me, "Isn't that your little friend we just passed?"

"What little friend?"

Her lips part in a big smile. "You know. The boy from the beach."

I jump up and look back. Kieran. Walking in our dust — head down, looking like somebody who hasn't any place to go. Out the rear window, he's growing smaller and smaller. I sink low again.

Roberta giggles. Her hand flaps at Phil's shoulder. "Let's go back and pick him up."

"*What?*" I say.

"Why?" says Phil with a quick, flat sideways glance.

"Poor boy is lonely," she says. "Come on, come on, turn around, we'll — *double-date!*"

Phil's startled eyes move back and forth between her face and the road. Her mouth is still open in a kind of alarmed smile at what she's just said. Then her whole expression begins to change. He's taken his foot off the accelerator. The car has begun to slow right down. A flicker of fear in Bobbi's big eyes. And then a challenge. Finally a soft kind of heat.

"Let me get this right," Phil says. "A date."

"Do you want to?"

He looks back at the road and lowers his voice, "You're

63

not a little girl, and I'm not just some guy. This isn't about just one date, Bobbi. We both know that."

"Do you?" she persists.

He looks back at her again and smiles.

"Turn the car around, please, Phil," she says.

Nervous flames lick high inside my stomach, into my chest, up into my throat. "We are *not* going back," I say, sitting straight up. "I will not be dragged off and used by you guys just because you're so hot for each other."

Nobody ever listens to me, of course. Phil lets the car come practically to a standstill and eats Bobbi up with his eyes and says, "I'm seven years older than you."

She answers quietly, "I know that, and if it doesn't make any difference to you, then it certainly doesn't make any difference to me." She brings down her arm and faces the road. "Turn around, okay?"

"Done." Hanging his cigarette out of the corner of his mouth, Phil wheels the car around right in the middle of the road. The tires spray gravel. We fishtail back to Kieran. When we sail past, he cranks his head to see who it is. Phil swings the car around. We speed right up alongside Kieran and come lurching to a halt.

"Cr-*ipes!*" I sink almost to the floor.

In the settling dust, Phil leans out the window and says in an excited friendly manner, "Hop in, stranger."

"What?" Kieran's voice, faint. "Oh. It's you."

"We're going to the dance at Crystal Lake," says Bobbi, leaning forward, looking past Phil out his window.

"Yeah?" says Kieran uncertainly. Both back windows are open. He peers in and sees me as I slowly rise up in the seat. "Hi," he says, eyelashes dipping down, hiding his eyes in the fast-growing darkness.

The flesh-colored moon seems as if it's riding on his shoulder.

"Come on," says Roberta. "There's nothing else to do in this place on a Saturday night."

"I was wondering what everybody did," he says, now looking full at me.

I don't say a word. I move over to make room for him, all the time staring out my window. He hesitates a bit, and then Phil swings open the door and pulls forward the seat. Kieran ducks his head and slides in beside me. His hair is wet, and some damp curls fall onto his forehead. I can smell the gum he's chewing. He eases his arm well up along the back of the seat so that his hand reaches behind my neck.

Phil drives us all toward Crystal Lake. Bobbi, clicking off the radio, settles back. They stare straight ahead, not talking.

I lean forward, elbows on my knees, looking accusingly at my still bandaged foot, chin in my hands. A couple of miles and a few zillion telephone poles go by.

Kieran finally leans forward, too, his hands dangling in front of him. He drops his head, cracks his knuckles. Slowly, he looks sidelong and just stares, his eyes pulling me in.

I turn and fumble with my window, rolling it up a few inches. I don't know what else to do, so I keep on rolling. Some of my hair whisks out. I roll the glass all the way back down. The evening air is wet and musky from all the reedy ponds that spot the dips and gullies in the miles of farmland between the two valley lakes.

"The reason I had to leave early last week," Kieran says finally, in a very soft voice, "was because I remembered I had to do something for my mom."

He fishes in his pocket. His jacket makes a swishing sound as he pulls out a piece of gum. He hands it to me, and a little tingle shoots right up my arm to my lips. My legs, quite suddenly, are mush. I look away so he won't see what I'm feeling.

12 ～☉～

The record changes. Sammy Turner comes on singing a slow, sexy version of "Lavender Blue," and it echoes clear up to the barnlike ceiling of the Crystal Lake dance pavilion.

Roberta and Phil are nowhere to be seen. As soon as we arrived, they were out on the floor under the dim lights, pretending to dance. What they were actually doing was standing tangled up in each other's arms and sort of weaving around on one spot. After that dance was over, he put his jacket around her shoulders, his hand on the small of her back, and then they got gobbled up by the crowd on their way out the back door to the beach.

The steamy hot place is packed with kids on the sidelines. Swaying bodies move out to slow-dance. Five tall girls who pulled up in a car with North Dakota license plates just as we got to the parking lot have just been jiving in the middle of the floor. Their pleated wool skirts are three inches above the knees. Dark navy knee socks, cardigan sweaters. They're all tanned, more or less blond, and showing off their new fall clothes in spite of the heat. They come off the dance floor giggling and sweating and talking all at once. A couple of town girls, whom I recognize from grade eleven last year, eye the short skirts — really disgusted — but I'd place bets that they'll go home and shorten their own for the opening day of school.

I've made myself scarce by the far wall. I'm sick of standing propped on my crutches, so I plunk down at the end of a low wooden bench beside us. Kieran moves over to stand up tall beside me. His arms are folded, his hands tucked under his armpits. Rocking slightly on his heels, he's faking it that he hasn't been watching a girl who graduated from grade twelve this June. Her name is Cindy Paget, and she's so popular that there are few people on this planet whom she lowers herself to notice. But she's certainly noticed him. Dressed in a low-cut red and green plaid cotton dress with a lace crinoline showing a quarter of an inch below the hem, she pushes by — deliberately brushing, face to face, up against him. He gives her a dumb, dazed smile. She has a Sandra Dee nineteen-inch waist, and she laughs over her shoulder as she wiggles her way through the sidelines.

I struggle with my damn crutches onto my feet.

"Do you want to go?" I ask Kieran.

Eyes still on her, he leans over. "What?"

"I need some fresh air," I say, and add pointedly, "I'm feeling a little sick."

"Where to?" He pushes away from the wall.

"The beach. There's a door at the back of the building."

68

On all sides the pavilion is open to the sandy beach, a park, the moon and stars, and Crystal Lake. We push along the sidelines.

I see two girls from Norton Crossings — stick-thin twins named Shiree and Shirae, who have large breasts, wear pointy brassieres, and who stopped going to school last year, only one week into grade ten. They'd just turned sixteen. We used to hang around together, nothing special.

Shirae whispers to her sister around the shoulder of her fiancé, Dave "Snortin'" Morton. As we pass, Shiree — giving Kieran the once-over — breaks away and says, "Sid! What have you been up to all summer?"

"Nothing much."

"I'll bet." She breaks into giggles. "Who's your friend?"

I sigh and stop. "Kieran this is Shiree, Shirae, and Dave Morton."

Once, when Shiree and I were younger, she yanked me into one of the girls' cubicles at school and asked me to look at her stomach.

"Why?" I asked stupidly.

"Because your dad's a doctor, and so you'd know," she said. Then, starting to cry, "I think I'm pregnant."

"How could you be pregnant? You're only twelve years old."

"I could," she sobbed, wrapping her arms around my neck. She smelled like mothballs and pepper and boiled cabbage. Their family is very poor. I hugged her and held her until she stopped crying and trembling. Then, finally, we both sank down to the floor, and I gave her a handful of sunflower seeds.

"Shiree," I whispered, "have you ever menstruated?"

"Have I what?" She looked at me, her face blotched and wet with tears.

"Have you started to get periods?"

"No," she sniffed, and spat out a sunflower husk.

"Well, then, you can't be pregnant. Girls don't get pregnant until they get their periods."

"Are you sure?"

"Absolutely a hundred percent certain."

That's when Shiree and I started hanging around together, followed soon after by her smarter sister. After that I learned a lot about life in general from being around them — watching Shiree, especially. Even in grade six, at recess, boys always wanted to horse around and sit on top of her. And one memorable night a couple of years ago, she persuaded me to get in the car with her and Kenny Matlock and Bernie Fife, who had just got his driver's license.

Bernie and I — thrill, thrill — kissed a few times in the front seat (I figured I might as well because I'd never been kissed before). But mostly we sat around and listened to the heavy breathing and moaning and jumping up and down that was going on in the back. Later, when he brought me home, Bernie got out of the car and hung around by the front door and mumbled a couple of million apologies for Shiree's and Kenny's behavior, and then said he hoped that it wouldn't affect how I felt about *him.* He's never been able to look me in the eye since, and after that I never went out at night with either of the twins.

Dave throws his beefy arms around the twins' shoulders and says, "Hi, Kieran. Actually, these are just a couple of chicks I picked up." He lifts his hairy forearm from Shirae's shoulder, scratches his head. "Don't exactly remember where, though."

"Yeah?" Kieran smiles, all teeth and tan, at Shiree.

Her eyes bright and shiny, she elbows Dave in the stomach and giggles harder.

"Oof," says Dave. "It's all coming back to me now."

Shirae says, "We saw Bobbi tonight."

"Yeah," says Shiree, rapidly chewing her gum. "Is her date Chinese?"

"Shiree, get a grip on your life," I say coolly, and push past them.

"Give me a call sometime," Shiree calls after me.

I struggle with my crutches through the crowd and push my way out the back door into the star-filled night.

Kieran comes out behind, then steps beside me, hands shoved into the pockets of his jeans. "First crowd I've seen since Toronto."

He walks slowly as I swing along through the park toward the small deep lake. Couples walk under the trees. Bobbi and Phil must have fallen off the edge of the world. They are nowhere to be seen.

"You'll have to get used to it," says Kieran as we get to the beach.

"Used to what?" I say sharply, looking at him.

"Just people — watching your sister and her boyfriend. They look different together, that's all. Don't get all huffy where there's no harm meant. You should relax more."

"I *am* relaxed." I try to face him. My crutches sink in the sand. I fight like a beached trout.

He laughs, coming around in front, taking my shoulders

71

to steady me. "Careful," he says. "Might break the other one."

"I didn't break it," I mutter. "I tore a ligament. And now it's hurting like hell, and I need to go home."

When we get back to the car, we discover Roberta and Phil. They sit up in a panic — Phil madly readjusting his untucked, unbuttoned shirt, Bobbi hastily pulling the zipper of her dress up past her unhooked brassiere.

13 ⟳

It's midnight. Over our heads, moths play suicide games with the bare bulb on our streetlamp. Kieran says, "I should probably walk you to your door."

Still sitting in our car, the streetlight reflecting off the red roof, Phil's face is already burrowed in Bobbi's neck. They want Kieran and me to disappear, and I'm in such a bad mood I want to blow up the car with them in it.

I swing away from Kieran and the light. He follows me across the sidewalk and the grass to the front door.

The midnight breeze off our lake whooshes and shivers through the dark branches of the fir trees. I flop down on the top step and heave my crutches off the side into the overgrown tulip bed. From my good foot, I pull off my white canvas shoe and chuck it onto the lawn.

"I'm just going to sit here for a while," I say, reaching down into the clump of ratty tulip leaves, pulling up a piece. I wave it around.

"You're not tired?"

"I never sleep until about four in the morning."

"Me neither. It's the only time I can really think properly. At night when other people are sleeping. So you're not going to go to sleep, then — I mean, not right away." He's hovering around as if he's in no hurry to go, as if he really wants to stay and be with me.

The night air is hot. The cement is cool. I don't want him to go either. I move over on the step.

He sits down beside me. Checks his watch. The bright moon peeks over the tops of the fir trees and lights his face, but not the watch. He kind of slumps over; his long fingers pull at the dark tufts of lawn around the front steps.

This silence is getting ridiculous. It's as though we're still both waiting for something.

I can't stand it anymore. "What time is it?" I say, and grab his wrist with the watch. Peer blindly at the shadowy dial. Turn up my face. Almost by accident my lips touch his ear.

He quickly turns and kisses me. Then his lips travel like sparks down my neck. They come back up across my jaw, my ear, my cheek, and then I find them again, hot and sweet all over mine. I don't want him to ever stop. He's breathing quickly, his hands in my hair. He pulls me tight against his chest. He kisses me harder. My arms are wrapped all around him, my hands in his hair, on his shoulders, down his back. I could just die, he feels so wonderful. His hand creeps under my blouse. He fumbles to get it under my brassiere. Then his hand is touching my breast.

"We should stop," I say, and I try to push him away.

74

"What?" he gasps.

"It's too fast."

He pulls his hand away and slips it around to my back. He's still holding me. He looks at me hard. Then he drops both arms. Turning from me, he quickly leans forward on the steps.

I stare at the back of his head, and tuck my hands between my knees, holding on to them. Then I lean forward to look at him. "Okay?"

He slowly nods his head and meets my gaze, his own startled eyes not blinking. Then we both sit up again.

We're side by side on the step, and I run my fingers along the rough cement. The silver moonlight is all, besides air, that's between us. It's like a silken thing. I don't know what to do next. And then I say, "Where were you last week? I mean, after the thing you remembered you had to do for your mother."

"Last week?" he repeats, as if he doesn't know what I'm talking about.

"You disappeared," I say softly.

He looks up at the moon. He slowly rubs his hands on his pant legs. Then he says, practically in a whisper, "I've already got a girlfriend, Sidonie."

I feel like I've just been hit by something that's hard and fast. If I stand up I may fall down again.

"Oh," I say.

"I'm sorry."

"Fine. I don't care."

He turns and looks at me. "Yes, you do. Don't say that you don't."

"Didn't you hear me? I just said — I don't care." I stand

up tall and dignified and icy. I manage to get inside the house. I slam the front door so hard behind me that I can feel the walls shake. And then my body goes all rubbery, and I sink down in the hallway and lean against a wall and stare and stare and stare at the moon that's coming through the window at the top of the door.

There were two moons last August — one that was almost full at the beginning when Mom was alive and our lives were normal, and then a big full cheater moon at the end, one that looked down so beautifully on the world when everything was awful and changed and never would be the same again.

14 ⟜⊚⟝

Mom's hands are full of white roses, and her skin is ice. I brush and brush her hair. It's night, and the moon is as flat and thin as paper, as thin as a child's cutout pinned onto a black curtain. The Ferris wheel bench squeaks back and forth. I look over to see the fields, but instead it's the lake. A dull light shines from a tall lamp-post, and around its base snow swirls and sweeps out across frozen water. Suddenly, my half of the bench gives way. And all at once I'm speeding away on a toboggan. The wind moans around my face. I look back and call for Mom. She's reaching out her arms — "You're dead, Sidonie" — and I'm hurtling farther and farther away from her, falling toward the deep dark lake.

I open my eyes and sit straight up at the end of the bed. My top sheet and blanket are heaped on the floor. I'm sweating and the mattress seems as big as an empty field and I feel like I'm shriveling up inside.

I pull up my pillow and rub it over and over on my sweaty face and down my chest. I hug the pillow flat against my body. I press my face against it. I hold the pillow tight and rock back and forth, back and forth. I'm wearing thin, cotton-lace shorty pajamas, and my legs are bare — except for the elastic bandage on my foot. It's too tight. I throw the pillow on the floor. I pry and twist at the two gold safety pins; my hands are shaking. I suck blood off my finger, unravel the bandage like crazy. Finally I'm rid of it. I scratch away at the skin on my anklebone — which is a roundish mound of yellowish mottled green. Running along the heel is a thin line of purple.

Someone outside has just started the spray hose. Water beads pelt against the house, the drainpipe.

The kitchen's screen door slams. Roberta's voice trails around the side of the house. "When do you want dinner, Dad?"

"Oh, Sunday time." He means seven o'clock. When Mom was alive, our ritual was to eat Sunday family dinners at seven o'clock. "Look at this garden. Do you think it needs fertilizer? What do you know about fertilizing roses?"

"Not much, but they'll probably wilt if the sun gets around to this side of the house before they dry off. Mom always watered them at night."

I guess he goes over to the tap and turns off the hose, because the water all of a sudden dies to a trickle. I hear it, soon, tapping Morse code on the ground.

I have to get out of this stifling house. I limp across the floor, putting most of my weight on my good foot. I throw on my Aztec-print flannel robe and fumble around with the waist tie.

78

Bogie follows me as I jump and hobble downstairs, through the shining hallway and out through the kitchen.

Mr. and Mrs. Coates's miniature poodle barks across the street. Bogie darts under the lilacs and follows me anyway, but hidden. We move around to the side of the house. The grass is soggy. The morning air hums with the sound of bees.

"Good morning, Muffet," says Dad when he sees me. "How's that ankle? Looks like it's healing pretty well."

He hasn't called me Muffet in about a year. I reach him and slip my arm around him, put my head on his rumpled shirt, and hug him tight. He smells of spicy after-shave, and I want to keep on holding him.

"Have a good sleep? It's a beautiful Sunday morning." He vigorously pats my back. A signal that I am dismissed.

"Phil's coming over for dinner," says Roberta, toeing the wet grass.

"Phil? Ah, good. Do you know if we have any fertilizer?"

"I think Mrs. North put some in the basement. What do you think of him?"

"Of who?"

"Phil."

"He's a very competent young man. I think he'll make a fine doctor. What do you think of him?"

"Oh. Well. I think he'll make a fine doctor, too."

I bend and shove my face into one of Mom's fully opened roses. The perfume is strong; the petals are cool and wet and soft as skin on my nose and lips.

Mrs. Coates shows up, in her church clothes, marching across our street. Her brat poodle yaps along beside her.

79

"Here comes that woman," says Dad. "She's going to ask us why we aren't in church."

Up close, she has a wide carnation-red face, large teeth, and (when she isn't caught spying) she's always wearing a la-di-da smile.

"Dr. Fallows," she shrills, waving her poodle away from her thick ankles.

"Oh, cripes," Dad mutters.

She arrives on our lawn and thunders through the grass in her sensible shoes. "I couldn't help but notice you out with your girls watering your wife's roses." She shakes her head sadly. Her baggy chin quivers. "Poor Eugenie."

"Yes," says Dad in a noncommittal tone. He bends down and rips up a dandelion.

"You really have to get at their roots," she says, "or they just take over. I'm always battling dandelions. They're such a nuisance." She looks coyly at Bobbi. "Well, Roberta, I noticed you parked under the streetlamp with your young man last night."

Dad turns a dazed look from the dandelion to Bobbi, who appears quite flustered.

"He's very nice looking for a Chinese," continues Mrs. Coates, prim as a tea cake. She holds her white handbag in her fat hands in front of her yellow shirtwaist dress. "I just stopped by, but I should be going now. Arthur, I see, is ready to go."

Skinny Mr. Coates, a tall graying man in his early sixties who wears the same brown tweed cap winter and summer, shuffles off their sidewalk onto the street and climbs into their dusty green Oldsmobile.

"Wherever is that Tommy?" She wheels around for the

80

poodle. Bum in the air, head under the lilacs, he's yapping at Bogie. His yaps end in a sort of strangled yelp. Bogie, I'll bet, has taken a swipe at him. The stupid dog never learns.

When Mrs. Coates leans over you can see the tops of her nylons. Tommy's legs kick at the air as she hauls him from under the bushes. She tucks him firmly under her flabby arm.

"And I notice Donina Stang's husband didn't make it home for the weekend again. Poor woman. I don't know how she manages without a man around the house. I'd be afraid to live alone. Especially in the kind of clothes she wears. Every inch revealed."

"Doris!" her husband calls from the driver's seat of their car. "We're going to be late for church."

"Oh, dear," she says with a meaningful look at all three of us.

Bogie swaggers out from under the lilacs, walks right over to her, and she backs up as if he's a rodent. Tommy starts in again.

"Just wanted to say hello."

"Very nice of you." Dad bares his teeth in a smile.

"Let me know, now, if there's anything you need. I'm always around." She walks away.

Bogie flips over onto his fat back and rolls around in ecstasy on the grass.

Dad watches Mrs. Coates, who turns and gaily waves. He politely raises his hand.

"Good-bye, Mrs. Coates," I whisper liltingly, "don't drive over a cliff or anything!"

"Sidonie, stop that," Dad says, and returns to his tooth-gritting smile.

"She's partially deaf," says Bobbi, also waving and smiling.

Mrs. Coates keeps right on waving as she sort of minces sideways. Tommy yaps and yaps and yaps and yaps.

"I wish," says Dad, "that somebody would kill that dog."

With a parting wave, Mrs. Coates stuffs Tommy into the Oldsmobile and loads herself in as well.

"Phil's a little old for you, don't you think?" says Dad. We all watch the car drive off.

"Only twenty-six, Dad," says Roberta, forcing a laugh. She rewinds a pin curl, crisscrossing it in place with two bobby pins, and adds, "Besides, we're just good friends. You know that you can't listen to anything Mrs. Coates says."

He looks at me, and I look at Roberta. And then he trudges off to the house — probably to locate the fertilizer.

"How long do you think you can get away with that one?" I say, following Roberta over to the lawn cart.

She picks it up and begins to carry it into the sunshine near the street. "I haven't the faintest idea what you're talking about."

"Oh, *come on.* The whopper you just told Dad."

She sets down the lawn cart. "I don't have to explain myself to you, kiddo."

"What's up with you, Bobbi?"

"I don't know what you mean."

"You're leading Phil on, aren't you?"

"For your information, *kiddo,* he's the only boy I've ever bothered to get to know first. They say best friends make the best lovers. Okay? Now, can I sit in the sun in peace and work on my tan?"

"Who says?"

She avoids my eyes. "I read it somewhere."

"Love, I'm sure, according to Leo Tolstoy." (Last month I read *Anna Karenina*, which was Mom's favorite book. I memorized the first line: "Happy families are all alike; every unhappy family is unhappy in its own way.")

I've touched a nerve, bringing Mom into the conversation in this way. I think she's going to cry. At least I've caught her attention. For once, at least, she isn't ignoring me as a person.

She places her hands on the back of the cart, leans in, calms herself, and says, "How do you think Dad would react if I wanted to marry someone Chinese — namely Philip?"

"I don't know. Phil's the best, Bobbi."

Her eyelids flutter up.

"Initially," I say, "he might blow a gasket. Then probably he'd ask if you could arrange to have the wedding on a Sunday so he wouldn't have to miss work."

Wrong thing to say. "Joke, okay?" I forgot that I can't jolly her along anymore. She's pretty unjollyable. I add, "Phil's brother, as we know, is anybody's guess."

"I'm from a good family," she mutters. "Dad being a doctor and all? At least I've got it half right."

She's such a chump. I think of Phil on the night of his dead mother's birthday. Of how it was Bobbi he'd wanted and needed to talk to. I just happened to be around.

"Roberta, if this is just another one of your little flings, I'll brain you. He's crazy about you, in case you haven't noticed. He could just go away. Do you want that to happen? All you have to do is treat him the way you've treated all the others."

"Phil and I *are* best friends," says Roberta, composed again. "He knows more about me than you or Dad or anybody." She lifts her nose and plunks down (heavily for such a small person) onto the lawn cart. "And he could go away anyway. That's just the way life is, and it's time you realized it."

"If Mom were here she'd tell you the same thing," I say. "*Think* about it. You break people's hearts, Roberta. You do it all the time."

Bobbi curls her lips. "*Don't* go bringing Mom into this — she's *dead.*" She closes her eyes tight and cranks her head away.

I am dismissed again. I can't even make her fight with me. So much for sisterly communication.

15 ⸺◎⸺

For three years that I can remember — when I was six, seven, and eight — Mom was fairly normal. She did things with the family, like the trip to Florida and, soon after that, the visit to Auntie Monique in the Qu'Appelle Valley. I hated the way everyone kept telling her how well she looked. It made me worry.

During the weeks before she came home from the infirmary, before her "well period," I was told she would need to rest a lot and I wasn't to tire her out. By the time she finally did come home, I didn't know what I was supposed to do. I even thought if I hugged her, it would hurt her. So I didn't. She thought I didn't like her. That was because every time she looked at me sadly I thought she was looking at me sickly, so I wouldn't even go near her.

That all changed one day when I came home from school. I had a reader about Dick and Jane, sappy Baby Sally and their wimpy cat Puff. The dad went to work every day wearing a hat, and the mom spent all her time baking cookies; they were actually a pretty boring family. I especially wanted to push Baby Sally (who couldn't do anything on her own) down a long hill in her little red wagon.

I came into the living room where Mom was sitting as usual, reading a nice thick book. I plunked down at the coffee table, took my scissors from their pencil case, and proceeded to cut Baby Sally to shreds.

"Don't do that!" Mom reached over and took the scissors. "Books are our friends. You mustn't cut them."

She'd been a teacher before she'd married Dad, just like her sisters were.

I flipped over to find Baby Sally on the next page. "She's such a poop," I said, taking a red crayon, scribbling all over her face.

"She's a nice baby," said Mom, horrified.

"She's a big fat poop," I said, smiling with satisfaction. My mother started to laugh. She didn't stop laughing for a long time. I think it was at that point that I became the family clown. As long as my mother was laughing, I figured, everything would be okay.

16 ──◎──

Donina Stang is sunning, fully clothed, on her front lawn. Well, relatively fully clothed. She's eating plums from a blue bowl set in the grass beside her, and her exotic nose is buried in a hardcover book called *Love for Lydia.*

She chews ravenously, while her brown eyes do a hundred-mile-an-hour scan of every line. She whips over the page. I walk across the street, hoping that Kieran will come out of his house next to Stang's, and knowing that even if he did I'd probably pretend to not notice him anyway.

My hair is still wet from the bath.

"Somebody ought to make a movie out of this book," says Donina, looking over at me. She pats the ground. Her nails are perfect almond shapes, and she doesn't paint them. I crumple up beside her. She puts down the book. "It's about a girl who ends up in a TB sanatorium. It's got love, pain, death, and sex — what more could you ask for? Want a plum?"

I love Donina. She speaks her mind. She treats me like a person. "Sure." I take one and bite into it. It's sweet and chewy.

"You sure smell nice, neighbor." She playfully twirls my soggy ponytail with her long fingers.

"Likewise," I say. "What's that terrific perfume?" (She likes to be complimented.)

"It's called Tabu. Only to be worn by women over twenty-five. You're in a bad mood." She leans back on her hands.

I drop back in the grass, sit up again to blow the plum pit into the street, and collapse once more. "My sister is a pain, and Mrs. Coates is a nosy old bat."

Donina has this deep throaty laugh. She's darkly tanned this summer; her skin gleams like some queen of Africa. "Mrs. Coates has nothing better to do than polish her floors and spy out her windows. And someday you and your sister will be friends."

"When hell freezes over." I help myself to another plum. But it's mealy and past its prime. I spit it out into my palm, throw it across the street, and drag my hand clean in the grass.

"Here." Donina dips her fingers into the bowl, scoops around, and comes up with a perfect moon-shaped plum, handing it to me as though it were a jewel.

"Thanks."

"Did you and Bobbi ever used to be friends?"

I shrug. "Back when there were dinosaurs and she was a real person."

"You have a good memory," says Donina, a trace of a smile appearing in her eyes. She raises one eyebrow. Settling back, she pulls her hair away from her neck, looks up into the sun, then back at me. She reaches out and gently squeezes the toes on my greenish foot. "I heard about this," she says. "Getting better?"

I shrug again and roll the warm plum around in my hands.

"We all keep our eyes on you, and we all worry — even if you don't think we do — including that funny old lady." She makes her eyes go enormous, crosses them, puckers her lips, and — putting her hand to the front of her face — pulls out a two-foot-long imaginary nose.

"Oh, I know that *she* keeps an eye on me," I say, smiling hard because she's being so kind and I feel like crying. "And you should hear her go on about *you*."

Donina smiles back at my ponytail. "When was the last time we trimmed your hair?"

"Two months ago."

"Want me to get the scissors?"

I nod my head and grin until my lips start to tremble.

She runs into the house and comes back soon with a sharp little bang of her back door. I sit cross-legged on her orange blanket in the sunshine while she kneels behind me and gradually unweaves the elastic to loosen my heavy wet hair. Then she begins brushing back from my forehead.

"You're getting to be such a pretty girl, Sidonie," she says, thoughtfully twisting my hair. "We should do this more often. I get lonesome, sometimes. Do you miss your mommy?"

I push on one side of the plum, softening and bruising it. Nobody's called my mom mommy in a very long time. I've suddenly lost my appetite for plums. I set it down on the blanket.

"I noticed," she says slowly, "that around the time she died, you started to look like a young woman on the outside. But you still sometimes feel like a little girl on the inside. Am I right? Sort of sad and scared?"

I don't want her to see that tears have started to spill down my face. But I want her to go on. I want her to keep telling me about my life, which seems to be in such a mess.

She continues to brush and smooth my hair. Even though she's stopped talking, I know she's carefully thinking of the next thing to say. I swipe the tears from my face. The brush bristles pull along my scalp, scraping over and over.

"So you have to find a safe kind of memory," Donina says finally, "to help tide you over the rough spots. For me it's a beautiful garden at night, and my grandmother and I have come outside to feel the breeze and smell the flowers, and she is talking softly to me in Hindi."

"Your garden in India?"

"Yes. Granny raised me until I was eleven and a half, and then my father sent me to school in England." She strokes and pats my hair. "And that's when I started to think about my grandmother and her garden at night. For a little while I could make England go away and be the happiest little girl again. Those feelings are still so strong."

I turn around. I feel a great surge of love for her. "You must have been so lonely in England. Did you ever get to go back — to visit your grandmother?"

She shakes her head. She threads her fingers through my hair, holds it out, examines it in the sunlight. I think that she may cry. She clears her throat and says, smiling, "My grandmother is an old woman. When she writes to me, she says that even though her new days are almost over, her old days are very good company. But still, she misses me as I miss her — with all my heart."

17 ⟳

This morning I've been working up the courage to go across the street — forty-five steps, if that — to call on Kieran McMorran. I'm thinking that maybe it's better to be miserable with somebody than to be miserable without them. Especially if that person kissed you even though he already has a girlfriend. Mom used to say, "Life is too short to worry about minor details." I was younger then and didn't have a full appreciation of what she meant.

I've finished making chocolate puffed-wheat candy and have set it on top of the stove. I pick off a corner and pop it in my mouth. Roberta's still in bed and has been there since seven-thirty last night. She's supposed to be at work today, but I heard her call in sick. Last night Phil didn't show up for dinner. No explanation from Bobbi. At the table she merely announced to Dad, "Phil's very sorry he can't be here."

"Oh?" Dad seemed relieved, but he must have seen her murky mood, because he ate two helpings of dried-out pork roast proclaiming that she's getting to be a better cook all the time. Trying to be a communicative parent, he then turned to me and asked if I had learned two Hula-Hoops at once yet.

"I learned to spin five at once about eight months ago," I said disgustedly, "and Wham-O's prices are down from two seventy-nine to fifty cents so they'll probably go bankrupt."

"Oh," he said, forlornly wiping his mouth with his napkin.

That sort of thing is just so hopelessly sad to watch. But where had he been for the past year? Was his brain in cold storage?

Still, I couldn't help but remember how he used to enjoy watching me try to spin those stupid hoops, before Mom died, so I muttered, "I also read somewhere that a Belgian expedition to Antarctica took twenty along," knowing that this little display of interest would make him happy.

"Is that a fact?" He smiled. "Have you finished reading *Walden* yet?"

Roberta quietly put down her napkin. "I'm going to bed now," she said. "I'm sure you two can manage the dishes."

Until Sunday night, my father hadn't dried a dish in about five years.

"What's wrong with your sister?" he asked as I handed him a soapy plate.

"Beats me." I shrugged.

"She seems" — he paused, slowly wiping, searching for the right word — "despondent."

"Yeah, well, we all get a little despondent from time to time. Around here it's practically normal." I dove in my hands for another dish, found a white coffee cup, flicked caked sugar off the bottom.

He took the cup, wrapping it around with the striped linen dish towel. He wiped and wiped. He didn't stop wiping until long after the cup was dry. And then he just held it and rotated it in his hand, frowning some more before he reached up and carefully placed it on the top shelf of the cupboard.

It would be nice to think that someday he could worry enough about us to actually do something about it. Last winter sometimes, he worried about me. I mean, he *looked* worried. And last night, I could see his glimmer of concern for Bobbi.

But this morning, as usual, he's off to worry about his patients. They are so much easier to worry about because they aren't angry with him for completely ignoring them.

I poke at the candy. It shines at me from the pan. The warm syrupy chocolate makes me remember Mom after school on a rainy March day. She cut Bobbi and me two big buttery chunks each (chocolate puffed-wheat candy was the closest she ever came to gourmet cooking). She sat at the kitchen table (chin in her hands — she looked so young, I remember now) to watch us and listen to us tell her about our day.

It rained all day, and Bobbi and Mom and I were still huddled around the kitchen table in our sweaters when Dad came home into the bright light from the wet outside — from the melting islands of drizzled-on snow and the infirmary, a three-minute walk away.

He carried his battered leather bag — full of chest X rays in brown paper sleeves, a couple of stethoscopes, patient progress reports in manila folders, business letters, and rattling glass bottles of medical samples. He opened the bag and hauled out about six colorful maps.

"What's this?" said Mom, fanning them out with a smile.

Dad leaned around and kissed her, and Bobbi and I covered our mouths with our hands and giggled. "A car trip to Florida, next month," he said, sweeping a fallen piece of shiny hair back from her shoulder. His hand stayed there as he added, "It's time this family took a vacation together."

So we went on a three-week car trip to Florida. I remember the ocean beyond the open car windows — the way it rolled back to the edge of the earth the way some wheat fields did back home.

I also remember being in the backseat with Bobbi. We'd pull strings of half-chewed gum out of our mouths and share it when we ran out of fresh stuff. Every once in a while, leaning over into the front, Bobbi would throw her arms around Mom, who was plump and pink and shiny from April right through to September that year. And all during the trip, we took turns climbing over the seat to be beside her — to play with her hair, her earrings, the gold cross on the gold chain that always hung around her neck.

At the end of every day there was a different motel and often a pool to swim in, where Dad would hoist squealing Bobbi onto his shoulders and cry, "Hold your nose!" before dunking her. With me, he played Father-Seal-Taking-Baby-Seal-for-a-Ride-on-His-Back as I clung to his neck and giggled. Each night we'd dress up to eat dinner at a family restaurant and, later, read one chapter and a poem. We got through the entire Winnie-the-Pooh collection, twice, from Canada to Florida and back again.

One night, in a motel with two bedrooms and a kitchenette, Bobbi and I heard a hissing staticky radio. We got out of bed and snuck a peek at Mom and Dad, who were dancing to some tune. He swung her around and sang to her in his monotone voice as her head fell back, as she laughed. I stuck my fingers in my ears. Bobbi pulled them out, leaned her chin on my head, hugged her arms close around me, and whispered, "Isn't she beautiful? Don't you think Daddy thinks she's the most beautiful woman in the world? She's all better now, don't you think? She won't ever be sick again."

Today it's raining just like that day that spring, when Dad came home and announced we were going to Florida.

I pull out a broad-blade knife from the right-hand side of the middle kitchen drawer. Nowadays the drawers are completely well ordered, which they never were while Mom was alive. Roberta's extremely neat. You can close your eyes, reach into any drawer, and pull out whatever you need. I miss seeing wads of string and knotted elastic bands with the cutlery. I cut into the puffed-wheat candy, lift a chunk from the pan. I wrap the sticky candy in waxed paper.

I pull on my plastic raincoat and step outside. The candy is a blurred shape inside one of the floppy clear blue pockets. Rain drips and plops all over me. My ankle aches dully as I trudge across the rain-perfumed street to Kieran's house.

It's a two-story brown clapboard, the oldest of the four houses on our street, with a screened-in porch and Virginia creeper almost reaching the screens. I run up the five steps to the porch door, open it, and step out of the rain onto the damp wooden floor. Four pairs of shoes neatly line either side of the brown bristly welcome mat. Looking left out to the valley road, I can see drenched green trees, and over their peaks the lake — whitecaps today. I tap on the door and wait. There's no answer. I knock a little harder. Finally I catch something moving behind the lace curtains of the little window on the upper part of the door. The door opens.

Tousled hair. Long tanned toes. He's pulling on a white shirt.

"Hi." He seems totally surprised to see me. One hand runs along his curls and stops at the back of his head.

"Could I come in?" I ask.

"Sure." He backs away from the door, shoulders kind of caved in, and shoves the other hand in his pocket.

"I made you some candy." I ease it out to show him. The waxed paper immediately unravels, revealing that one side of my gift has sagged off. I try to pinch it back together. "I didn't know if you liked chocolate — or puffed wheat for that matter. See? There's the puffed wheat. That's what all those little bumps are." I know I'm starting to babble and I could just die, but I can't make myself stop. "You cook it up with butter and corn syrup and vanilla and cocoa . . . well, actually you add the puffed wheat after . . . I mean, after all the liquid stuff is cooked, you put it in. That's when you add the puffed wheat, see? There it is . . ." Shut up, Sidonie. Shut up, shut up, shut up. With a

97

sickening sinking feeling I add, "It's pretty easy to make."

"I've made it before," he says, looking confused.

"Oh. You have?" My gift is a disaster. If there is a hole in this floor, please let it swallow me up. "Of course you know, then, how it's made."

He picks up the candy. "It's still warm," he offers, standing there examining it.

"That's the best way. Warm." I don't know what to do next and I don't want this conversation to be over, but I can't think of anything else to say. I turn away. "I guess I'll go now. Enjoy your candy." I start to pull up the hood of my raincoat. I reach for the door.

His hand appears and covers mine. "Don't go."

My hood drops back onto my shoulders. My hand freezes under his on the metal doorknob.

He says, "I walked out on you the other day, when you hurt yourself, because . . . well, you and your dad . . ." His voice trails off.

I turn around and can't meet his eyes, so I stare at his bare feet as he's clinging to my hand.

He says in a firmer voice, "My dad would have told me to go home and stop whining. He's a bit of a bastard."

"My dad and I aren't especially close," I say, lifting my eyes.

"Sure seemed like it." He smiles that terrific quick smile of his, and then it disappears and he says seriously, "I have to explain about Saturday night."

My heart is sinking fast. I don't want explanations. His hand is so big that mine is completely wrapped inside. I start to pull away, but he's still holding on. I'm afraid that I'll cry, make a fool of myself again.

"I made it for you — the candy. I made it just for you," I start to babble again, "because it's a rainy day, you see. I thought maybe you might be missing Toronto and everything. Because it's raining."

I don't know what to say. I don't know where to look. I don't know what to do. If he wanted to, he could crush me with a single word.

"It's okay," he says, moving so close I can feel his breath in my hair.

Then suddenly he's pulling me, dripping raincoat, muddy shoes, and all, past the living room, down the front hallway. I am whisked around a corner into their brightly lit kitchen. It smells of chicken and some kind of unidentifiable spice.

He slides out a chrome chair from a pale yellow Formica table and steers me into it, one hand on my shoulder. I sit.

From a cupboard with little red wooden knobs he gets out two tall glasses. He goes to the refrigerator, pours us some orange juice. He comes back, sets the glasses down on the table, and slides into a chair, pulling it closer to me. I watch him break the puffed-wheat candy into two even pieces.

Not talking, we sit and pick away at the sweet warm candy. It stops raining. Just a few odd drops clatter onto the tin eaves outside.

In a little while, he says, "It's quiet here. Not like the city and all that traffic. Not like Toronto. I like your skies. All those Bible story sunsets — you know the kind where you can almost see a big finger coming out and pointing at you?"

I feel as though someone just took a knife and scraped down the inside of my heart, leaving it clean but too raw to touch. "That's exactly what they look like," I say, smiling and smiling. I want his voice to keep on, running from one day into the next.

"And the stars," he continues. "There's so many of them. Just a zillion white stars. Better than at a planetarium. Reminds me of this lake just east of Toronto. Rice Lake. We bought a cottage there a couple of summers ago. Had some pretty good times. Dad also bought a sailboat. For about a week we spent every day out on the lake. He taught me how to sail — more or less."

"Will you know soon if you're staying?" I break in. Then I back off: "Just wondering."

"You mean to live?"

"Yes." I casually drop my head to the juice glass. My mouth is dry. My top lip sticks to my teeth.

"Actually, I've been *living* out of a suitcase for the past three months."

"Oh?"

"Ever since Mom moved away."

"Oh."

I watch him drum his fingers on the table. He rocks back on his chair. He comes forward again and stares into his glass. "Her old job at the Toronto General is still there if she wants to go back at the end of September. Or she might stay," he adds quickly. "They've offered her a permanent job here, if she wants it." He slowly cracks one of his knuckles. He does this twice. "Everything's pretty much up in the air."

"So that's in about two months — if your mom goes back," I say carefully. "Will you start school here?"

"That's the plan so far. I live from one plan to the next." He suddenly smiles. "Had this summer job with my buddy, Mike Hoogstraten? Lifeguarding." He swirls the orange juice around in his glass, drinks some. Wipes the corners of his mouth with his thumb and forefinger. His eyelashes shade his eyes. "But halfway through it got pretty weird. Mom was gone, and most of the time I stayed over at Mike's." He continues in a sudden rush, "Dad hardly ever showed up." He pauses. "Mom just thought it'd be better if I came here for a while. I guess you could say he's sick."

"Mom was sick, too," I blurt out.

He looks up. "Alcoholic?"

"No — no, nothing like that."

"Oh." Another pause, and then, "I didn't know she'd died." He adds quickly, "I sure felt stupid the other day."

"That's okay."

"Mom told me later that it happened about a year ago."

My mother's death has always been a guaranteed conversation stopper. "My mom died of heart failure," I say. A failed heart. Failing hearts. "She was sick most of my life. It's not like we weren't expecting it."

I wonder what he's going to do now — change the subject? Or will he just let it hang in the air and then say something stupid? I wait for what will happen next. He just sits there, taking in this information, like he did when he first saw my hurt foot. Like he's examining some sort of injury that you could actually see.

"That would be hard on everyone," he says at last, in a quiet way. "Especially if she was sick for a long time." He's staring at his glass now, rubbing his fingers up and down the water beads that have collected on the outside. "I really seriously have to tell you something, Sidonie," he says, right out of the blue.

I don't want to hear it. I plunge ahead. "There's this place I used to go when I was really worried about her. In the woods — quiet. Think you'd like it, and I haven't been back for quite a while. Want to go?"

He's searching my face as if he's memorizing it. "Sure," he says. "Sure, I'll go."

18 ─◎─

The rain has temporarily cooled down the valley. There's a rush of freshness that comes, like suddenly letting air inside a sealed jar. But the sun has come out hot as ever.

"It's down *here?*" asks Kieran in front of me.

He stops on the little overgrown path. Through the leafy trees the sun dances in little spots on his back. I'm close enough to feel the heat rising from his skin through his T-shirt. "Just keep going," I tell him.

"Cripes, this is a jungle," he says, winding along in front of me on the foot-wide trail.

I put my hand on his back to give him a playful push, but it sticks there like a magnet. I can feel his shoulder blades, the muscles tightening across them. "Just a leaf," I say, awkwardly brushing off his shirt.

He startles me by turning around, catching my hand

between his. I'm laughing, and he spins around again. "Get up on my shoulders," he says, looking back.

"What!"

"Yeah, do it." He crouches down, pats his shoulders.

I climb on, feeling giddy and a little scared. He's so tall, and in addition to being terrified of deep water I am also somewhat nervous of heights.

He lifts me up. "How's this? Nice view?"

The treetops seem to spin all around us.

Looking over the top of his head, I can see this big terrific grin spread all over his face. "God, you're small," he says.

"Just follow the path," I say, laughing. I lock my arms around his face, his chin. I want to bury my face in his warm sweet hair. As we slip down the path he hugs my legs closer down around his body and I feel weak.

The loud burbling of the creek and the cool there rise straight up when we get to the bottom of the ravine.

"We're here," I tell him.

He uses one arm to steady me as I slide down his back. His other arm comes around me. My feet touch the ground. And then, somehow, he's holding me, and I'm holding him. My cheek is pressed against his soft T-shirt, his chest.

"This girl. In Toronto. She's Mike's sister," he mumbles, as if his tongue has suddenly gone numb. "She's my best friend's sister."

He squeezes me tighter, and I'm hanging on to him.

"I've practically lived at their house for the past five years," he says. "At parties, Dr. Hoogstraten even introduces me as his other son."

104

He moves one hand up and down my back. I can hear his heart beating fast. I can feel it behind the soft white cloth. I push my ear closer. I want his heartbeat to drown out everything else.

"Lenore's had this big crush on me for a long time," he whispers. "And at the beginning of summer, she caught me in a kind of a weakened state after Mike and I got home drunk one night from a beer bash. I made a big mistake. I let her keep on thinking that we had something going."

He takes me by the shoulders and slowly holds me away, "Dr. Hoogstraten told me during one of our 'little chats' — and he's *real* fond of having little chats — that sometimes life gets so crazy the only thing that makes any sense is just to be honest with people. Sidonie, let me finish — "

I pull away. I quickly plunk down on the creek bank.

"He's very big on loyalty," Kieran says, and he comes and sits down beside me. He looks hopelessly all around. "Everybody, including his own son, respects him, and he's been better to me than my own father. If it weren't for the whole family, as a matter of fact, I don't know where I'd be. I just can't do anything to mess that up. Don't you see the kind of a bind I'm in?"

I don't answer him. I feel as if somebody just handed me a million dollars and then snatched it away again.

"So this is — the place," says Kieran heavily. "Ever throw in pennies?"

"Pocketsful," I say, sagging my chest over my knees. "Even, once, a quarter. I was in a bit of a bind, myself. It was one of the times when Mom was really sick. I was pretty young. I thought wishes could make her healthy."

I'm thinking over and over: I'm not going to let you go. Not now. I'm not going to let you go.

I say, "Okay, we won't."

"What?"

"We just won't."

"We won't what?" he says. "See each other?" He rolls over on his side in the cool moss.

"What I mean is we'll be friends."

"Friends?"

"I don't have one. Never have had one. Not somebody I could really talk to. Why not be friends?"

"It wouldn't work," he says, sitting up again.

"Where's the rule that says we can't be friends?" I say desperately. "Who else are you going to talk to here, anyway? Norton Crossings is five miles away. Crystal Lake is fifteen. Haven't you noticed that this place is practically a desert island? Do you have your driver's license?"

"Got it before I came here. My birthday's in June. But right now it's pretty well useless to me. Mom says there's no sense buying a car until we know where we stand."

"I've got a car. But no driver's license. We need each other."

"Your dad wouldn't ever let me drive your car."

"It isn't my dad we'd ask. It's my sister. She runs the show."

"*She* does?"

"Dad's always working, and he leaves most of the deci-sions up to her."

He thinks about this for a bit. He has a habit of biting down on his teeth and flexing his jaw muscles. He says, "You're kidding me — you've never had a friend?"

106

"Never."

"Not *ever?*"

"Nobody my own age," I say, thinking of Phil.

"But what about those twins we met at the dance?"

"I went to Norton Crossings School with them. I just hung around with them. They weren't my buddies or anything." I pick up a small white stone and slowly roll it over and over between my hands. "So what do you say?"

The sun barely makes it all the way down here — spinning through branches and leaves. I pull off my shoes and socks. I dangle my feet in the creek and wait for his answer.

We both see a spotted leopard frog as it jumps off the shallow bank and swims down into a pool of water that's pale as tea. A column of sunlight follows it and then, legs kicking, it disappears somewhere between two rocks. Algae flows out between them, like dark green hair. The water slowly slips away. I spot a dark brown penny at the bottom that didn't disappear in last spring's torrents of melted snow water.

"You mean," Kieran says, "we'd *just* be friends."

"Not *just*," I turn to him. " 'Just' means not important."

"This doesn't make sense," he says, shaking his head. "Sidonie, how could we be friends? Even at music camp they have this really hopeless rule: girls and guys can't ever be any closer than a foot apart. That way they don't touch, supposedly. God knows who thought up that one. He must have been a monk with an IQ of 10. In everyday life, when two people like each other, that doesn't work."

The wind slightly stirs the tops of trees so dizzily high

above. I look down and point out a spiky rusty-red flower on a thread-thin stem. It daintily pokes up between us.

"We'll make it work," I say. "It'll work. Don't you want it to work?"

"I do." He touches the flower with his finger. "I just don't think it *will* work."

"But you *do* want it to."

"That's not the point."

"Promise me."

"This isn't logical," he says, lying back, folding his arms across his chest.

"Lots of things aren't." I ease down onto my elbow. "If they were, we'd all be really interested in mathematics. Billions of people would suddenly be rushing around trying to figure out equations that would show them why life isn't usually very fair."

He sits up again, studies his feet. "You're the most intelligent girl I've ever met," he mutters. "And you're also the craziest."

He tosses a little tuft of moss into the creek. "All right, maybe we could be friends," he says at last. "Okay. Friends."

I sigh with tremendous relief. I lie fully back and run my hands along the cool moss.

Kieran leans forward. He restlessly picks out little bits of gravel from between the soles of his moccasins. His body jerks with the movement as he tosses them away. "Why did you stop coming down here?" He looks back at me. Then he returns to the wedged bits of gravel.

I can't answer him. This is too hard to talk about.

The day my mother died, I remember finally coming up

from the ravine and walking across the lawn into the dark kitchen. I remember seeing, with a shock that sent my heart racing, her clear blue hairbrush still faceup on the kitchen table, still tangled up with strands of her long hair, and Roberta upstairs, sobbing, and Dad, empty-faced, slumped in his chair in the living room. I pulled out that clump of hair. I smoothed it and twined it around my finger and wound it into a tiny ball. I thought at least it would be something, some piece of her to keep. But a few months later I threw it out. Without her, it didn't mean anything.

19 ⟿

On the last morning of her life, my mother got up and made pancakes for breakfast. They turned out to be another of her culinary failures; she burned them. But I ate one anyway. It was the least I could do — even if it *was* raw in the middle.

Later, she sat by the open kitchen window in her dressing gown, and that's when I redid her hair in a French roll and made jokes I had no heart for while Roberta angrily scraped the gooey, blackened torn-at pancakes off the plates into the garbage.

Dad, kissing the top of Mom's head, rested one hand briefly on her shoulder. She touched his hand just as he pulled away.

Then we all left her. Dad to the infirmary for the morning rounds of his patients. Roberta and I in the old blue Chevy for the fairgrounds at Crystal Lake.

A few days later at the graveyard — a little Protestant

cemetery on a hill above Norton Crossings — Auntie Monique stood on the other side of the grave from our family. Auntie Lucille was somewhere on a ship on the Atlantic Ocean, on her way back from France, where she had been teaching for a year, and Dad had sent her a telegram. But Monique was here, looking at her feet and crying. Roberta and Dad didn't cry. They didn't touch each other either. They stood side by side, each a kind of reflection of the other's profile. I'd never felt so lonely. I wanted to be with Monique. I wanted Mom's sister to put her arms around me. I started to think about her Qu'Appelle Valley kitchen when I was eight and Mom was alive.

It had a wood-burning stove. It had two big windows looking out to a yard that had gooseberry bushes and raspberry canes and vegetables and clumps of old-fashioned-type flowers with names like larkspur and mignonette and coralbells.

And all that week Auntie Monique and Mom dragged out old family photo albums and laughed over pictures of themselves from fat babies right up to the hairdos they wore when they were young women in their twenties. At night we played Crokinole on the kitchen table until it was late and Bobbi and I were finally sent off to bed.

Our bed had gray metal balls on fancy scrollwork for the headboard, and the mattress was high off the floor. Bobbi had to hoist me onto it. We pulled over us a quilt that was made by some woman who collected old clothes and rags and cut them up into patchwork. It was heavy and warm and smelled of lavender. Until Mom and Auntie Monique had finally left the kitchen — while we could still hear them laughing and gabbing back and forth in both French and English — Bobbi, in the dark, would tell me stories she made up on the spot about this impoverished girl who had TB and was actually a princess in disguise. Horrible things happened to her, like the time she had to eat bats to stay alive, but she always triumphed in the end.

I loved those stories. They were the best.

It's funny what you remember about people. The smell of somebody's kitchen (Auntie Monique, unlike Mom, was a fantastic cook), picking saskatoon berries in the morning when the cold dew still wets your pant legs, or just something like fingers stroking the edge of a coffee cup, can make a whole person appear in your mind's eye. Almost as if they had just stepped out, in full Technicolor, in front of you.

Mom and Auntie Monique weren't particularly alike except for a few things. They were almost the same height, the same dark coloring. And there was something about their eyes, the way they smiled with them, and especially about the way they used their hands.

People lowered my mother's coffin into the grave. There were prayers and a shovelful of dirt. I closed my eyes and shivered, but I didn't cry. I pulled my hands inside the ski sweater Mom had given me for my fifteenth birthday. And then I started to think about how I'd missed the chance to say something important to her by not being there when she needed me. When she was dying. I hugged myself and wanted to die, too. I wanted her back again. I wanted her arms around me. I wished for it so hard that I actually thought I could feel her arms come from behind. She squeezed so hard it almost took my breath away. I kept my eyes closed. I didn't want the magic to go and disappear on me.

Sometimes I'll pull the family photo album out from our dining room buffet, open wide the worn brown leather cover. The pictures, many of them the same as Monique's, aren't important to me because they show Mom and her sisters in their early life. They're important because they remind me of that week we all had together. That's the kind of memory you want to hang on to.

20 ⟋⊚⟍

Something is definitely amiss with Roberta. Phil has totally dropped out of the picture, and this morning she's playing sick again, wrapped up like Mom in her morning robe and slumped over a cup of coffee at the kitchen table.

"What's up?" I say, dumping myself down in the chair across from her.

"Nothing." She drops her head, sipping the bitter-looking sludge.

"Okay." I get up. "If you don't want to tell me, then don't."

"He hasn't called."

"Who hasn't?" I know perfectly well who.

"He's avoiding me like I've got leprosy or something."

"There go my eyeballs," I sing, sitting down again, *"into the highballs."*

"Do you always have to be so amusing?" she says, getting up and going over to the sink.

"So why isn't he calling you?" I reach over to grab three sugar cubes out of the sugar bowl. I shove them into my mouth.

Her back, that's what I get. Her stupid back as she leans against the sink. I want to scream.

I walk out of the kitchen. I go into the living room, over to the telephone on the dark oak side table by the hi-fi.

A shaft of dust-speckled morning sunlight falls across the piano's black and white keys. (Before Phil came along nobody played it, except, of course, Grandma Fallows, who died before we were born, and also Bobbi and me long ago when we were forced to take lessons.) At the moment it's back to its original function, as a piece of furniture.

I'm going to call Kieran. I'm so glad to have somebody to phone now, just to say hello.

Except that that might have all kinds of potential meanings, and I shouldn't appear eager. Point in fact: we didn't say good night last night until absolutely the last minute he was supposed to be in — at midnight. It's a good thing I don't have a curfew. It's a good thing nobody's ever bothered to give me one.

The phone rings. I practically jump off the floor. I pick up the receiver.

"Hi," says Kieran. "I know it's you."

"What?"

"I saw you standing by the phone. I saw you from the porch."

"God." I laugh, nervous, thrilled. "Have you been spying on me?"

"I left a message for you on my porch steps. Can you see it?"

I turn and look out the window. He's made a big sign out of cardboard — like a picket sign. It's sort of wobbly looking, shoved between the wooden steps. "It's kind of faint," I say, trying to make out what it says.

"Used my fountain pen. You can't read it?" he says, disappointed.

"No."

"It says: Good morning, buddy."

I burst out laughing.

"Do you like it?" he asks.

"I do — I do! I love it. It's nuts. You're nuts. Thank you."

"You're welcome," he says, really pleased. "So what are you doing? Do you want to come out?"

"I do — yes!"

I roar upstairs and change into something that's clean and not too obviously great looking. Then I come crashing downstairs again to the front hall. I sit on the floor to pull on my sneakers and tie the laces.

I get up off the floor and call, "I'm going out now."

Bobbi doesn't answer. I know she's still in the kitchen. But she's not making a sound. Not moving. She's always moving. She's always working. This isn't like her. Maybe I should stay and talk to her.

"Bobbi?"

Silence.

"Fine, then, ignore me," I mutter, and slam the front door behind me.

Kieran's across the street sitting on his steps, twirling the sign he made between his big tanned hands.

I walk across the gravel. I'm so glad to see him, but I'm starting to feel so lousy about Bobbi that I put on a Doris Day smile, one that's hooked to each ear.

"You and your sister have a fight?" he asks.

"No," I lie, holding on to my smile.

He eases the sign off the side of his steps and onto the grass.

"Want to walk it off?" he says, and gets to his feet.

"What off?"

"You're upset. I can tell," he says, lightly placing his hand on my elbow. "So let's go for a walk."

We get onto the street and start walking toward the lake. His hand strays down my elbow. I take it and hold it, just being friendly, skin against skin. I may possibly melt.

"Inch apart," we say, practically in unison. He squeezes my hand before he lets go.

"Must have been lots of frustrated people at your music camp," I say lightly.

"Not so you'd notice." He laughs. "People were always sneaking around at midnight. Behind the canteen. Under the stage. Out on the lake in boats."

I sneak a look at his profile. He catches me looking.

"I wasn't one of them of course."

"Oh, of course." I laugh, pushing his shoulder with my hand.

He pretends to lose his balance and goes staggering off down the lake road.

I run after him. "What kind of instrument did you play?"

He spins around, quickly walking backwards. "Drums. I'm really good."

"I'll bet you are," I say, and he lets me catch up.

"Why?" He stops. It's a serious question.

"You listen to Art Blakey."

"Oh." He shuffles his feet. "That."

"You've got great taste. He's the most. Did you bring them with you?"

"What?"

"Your drums."

He starts walking again. "I don't have them anymore. Dad came home and put his fist through the skins a couple of weeks ago when I was going shack on them. And then he kicked them around pretty good. They aren't worth fixing."

"Why did he do that?" I say, appalled.

"That's Dad." He shrugs.

"I'm sorry," I say, taking his hand again.

"Don't, okay?" He pulls away.

"I'm just sorry — that's all." I walk slightly ahead, under the hot sun. "Can't a person show that they're sorry?" I pull a frayed string from my pocket. Dust swirls around my ankles. I tie up my hair. By the roadside is a long line of poplar trees that look like human ribs. I feel Kieran's hand come riding up along my shoulders. He makes me stop.

"You're the prettiest girl I've ever known," he says, slowly stroking me, his unsmiling profile against the trees, the lake. His hot hand on my skin is as electric as lightning across a prairie sky.

"How about Lenore Hoogstraten?" I say, jealous, confused.

118

He lifts his head high and we walk on toward the beach. He lets his hand slip from my shoulders. In the pocket of his shirt is an expensive-looking tortoiseshell fountain pen with a gold clip. The one, I guess that he used to write his message to me.

We follow tire ruts in the grasses off the road down toward the beach. Turquoise damselflies fly up around us like jewels in the air. I stretch out my hand. One darts and swoops; it lands, as graceful as a ballerina, on the tip of my finger.

"Look!" I turn to show it to Kieran. "Dragonflies always keep their wings spread, but damselflies fold them back like shiny skirts."

His eyes reflect the sunlight and water. "Do you want to know why Phil is staying away?"

I wave my hand. Wave the thing off.

"How would you know?" I say casually. "You don't even know him. Not really."

Kieran comes to a dead stop, working his fingers, his hands, in and out of nervous fists. He walks away down onto the beach. I follow him. I wish he weren't so moody all of a sudden.

I watch him pick up a bulrush that's washed onto shore. He starts twisting it out of shape. He sits down. He works away at the bulrush, pulling it into shreds, putting the shreds through a series of practiced-looking sailor's knots.

"How would you know about Phil?" I sit down beside him.

Kieran stands up and dusts the shale and sand off his pants. "I've got eyes. I notice things. Don't you care that he might not be coming back?"

"He's coming back."

"Maybe he isn't."

"I don't see why it's any concern of yours."

"Why don't you want to know?"

I don't want to tell him why. I don't want to tell him that I can sometimes get so depressed I feel like throwing up.

Kieran stares moodily out at the lake, to the dark green hills a couple of miles away on the other side. "Maybe he's got himself into a situation that's too hot to handle," he says. "And he's afraid that she's just a big flirt."

"She *is.*"

"If it's only some dumb summer romance for her, then he probably thinks that it's not worth busting his balls over." He stands still and brooding, not even blinking. He's waiting. Waiting for his words to gradually sink in.

I am absolutely stunned. "Who are you talking about — them or us?"

He towers over me, working his jaw muscles, looking down as if he's ready to explode. Finally he says, "I'm just testing you. I don't think that you're sincere."

"Sincere? What do you mean sincere?"

His eyebrows hood his eyes.

"You don't think *I'm* sincere?" I can't believe this. I can't believe him. I get to my feet. "Go to hell." I start to walk away.

He sticks out his arm, catching me. I push against it with all my strength, until he lets it drop.

I walk, then run, back up to the road. At the top, I pull off my sneaker and pour a thin trail of sand out of the heel. He's still down there by the water. He bends and picks up a

120

piece of shale. With a strong, angry swipe of his arm, he hurls it like a shooting star across the still glassy surface. It touches down one, two, three, four times, leaving rippling circles that widen and cross over themselves so quickly I can't even tell which one is which.

I shove my shoe on my foot. Hot tears run down my face. I walk away, fast. I feel a burning pain growing steadily inside me. I have to walk far enough and fast enough so that this pain won't suck me down.

21 ⟶◎⟶

Saturday, August the fifteenth. Today is my six-teenth birthday. Will this be my lucky year? Last year, on this very day, my mother died.

It was for my birthday that she got up and made those pancakes. Shuffled around in furry slippers and her blue coffee-stained quilted dressing gown, the gold cross that she never took off (it's Roberta's now) on the chain around her neck. Spooned watery-looking pasty stuff into a black frying pan. Served it up with a discouraged sigh. Only Mom could ruin a pancake mix.

She reached over with her fork, lifting the crispy charred edge of one of mine. "Do you think they're good, Sidonie? No, I guess not. Eat nearer the middle. The maple syrup is nice. All the way from Quebec. You're too thin."

"I love them, Mom. They're unusual."

"Raw. In some places."

"All the great chefs are French." I dragged out the old family joke.

Her large eyes quickly filled with tears.

I shoved another piece in my mouth. I figured even if I gagged on the damn things I would eat them. I said, with my mouth full, "They taste *wonderful*, for Pete's sake."

"I didn't even pick out your present," she said.

Roberta got up from the table and dumped her own pancakes into the garbage.

"You told me what to get, Eugenie," said Dad, who doesn't eat breakfast except on Sundays. He sipped his morning coffee. "You gave me explicit instructions."

"The sweater's really nice, Mom."

"It goes well with your coloring, I think."

"Black is totally inappropriate for a fourteen-year-old." Roberta's hands were already shoved deep into sudsy dishwater.

Mom sat there looking as if Bobbi had slapped her.

"*Fifteen*," I said. "And I like the color. It's sophisticated. Bobbi, can't you just shut up?"

Dad got up and dropped his cup into the dishwater.

Mom said, "You haven't tried it on yet." Her tired eyes followed me as I stood up from the table.

"I will later, okay? Bobbi's promised to take me to the fair at Crystal Lake as her birthday treat." I glared at Bobbi.

"That's very nice of you, Bobbi," said Mom, smoothing the edge of the tablecloth. She wore her long hair (not even a hint of gray) in a single braid at night.

Bobbi shook soapsuds out of her hands. They splattered all over the wall behind the sink. "Let's go," she said. "Let's get out of here."

Before Mom died, Bobbi and I were still semifriends. Things were so tense at home, and she was always taking me places where the two of us acted like escaped jailbirds. We'd drive at dangerous speeds, singing at the top of our lungs to radio tunes. The car would fishtail over the soft gravel roads. We'd never just go to Norton Crossings. We went as far as we could go, to Crystal Lake. The store-keepers there hated us. We never did anything really bad, but we always looked and acted reckless. In the drugstore Bobbi, shaking with giggles, painted clown faces on me with tester tubes at the Maybelline counter. In Olman's Groceteria, I'd get into the grocery cart and pretend I was her brain-damaged sister. I'd make horrible noises and drool at customers while she, straight-faced, flung boxes of cereal and Kleenex and rolls of toilet paper on top of me.

Then we'd come home and practically be strangers again.

Only a few days in that last year was Mom able to rally around and try to be like her old self. My birthday was one of them. I had to choose the day she died not to show her how I looked in that hot, thick, very expensive black sweater with the white and red skiers endlessly crisscross-ing a path around the cuffs and waistband and neckline.

22 ⟋⊙⟍

Maybe Bobbi's just forgotten today's my birthday. I take her breakfast upstairs on a tray. I tap lightly on her door. I'm wearing the sweater Mom gave me over my shorty pajamas. It's nine o'clock. I need to talk.

I set down the tray in her darkened room. "Roberta," I say, lightly shaking her.

She draws a loud breath, rolls over, opens her eyes.

"Hi," I say. "I made your breakfast."

"God, it's hot in this room. Why are you wearing a sweater?"

"Sit up." I pull at the pillow behind her head.

She sits. I fluff the damp pillow. Place it, and another, behind her. She leans back.

I go to her window, pull the blind, open it all the way. The rose-sweet morning air rushes in.

I go back to Roberta, pick up the tray, and set it on the bumps her legs make under the sheets. She stares at her

125

breakfast, and I sit on the edge of the bed. Picking up her spoon, she begins to dig around in the Rice Krispies. The bright white milk drips back into the bowl as she lifts the spoon to her mouth. With no red lipstick, she looks about twelve years old. She slowly chews, swallows, sets down the spoon.

"This is very nice of you," she says almost shyly.

I want her to say happy birthday. I want it to be ten years from now, away from this sadness that always hits us. I want us to be friends again.

She plays for a while with the Rice Krispies, but I can see she isn't going to eat any more. I pick up her tray. She raises her eyes and doesn't protest. I put the tray down on the floor. Hand her the cup of coffee.

"Drink it," I say.

She just sits there, holding it.

"Come on, Roberta." I lift it up.

She begins to drink.

"*All* of it."

She downs it. I take the cup and put it back on the tray by my foot.

I say, "I know you're sad about Phil. And maybe you don't want to talk about that. But is this about Mom, too?"

Roberta chips away the red polish on her thumbnail. "It isn't easy being the oldest."

"I know. I guess that's why you act like you're in charge of everything."

Her hand is shaking. "I don't know what else to do." Little pings of polish, like red sand, fly all over her blanket.

"Just be yourself, Bobbi. And don't try to be her. You can't be Mom."

126

"I've never wanted to be that. Do you think all this has been my choice?"

This is one of the saddest things she's ever said to me. I could say something else, get her to talk about what it is she wants from this family, but I don't. Instead, I sit like a lump.

She starts to twirl a lock of limp hair. "Did you ever say, 'I love you, Mom?' "

"No. I just thought it. I never said it."

"She died all alone. It should never have happened."

"Over her second cup of coffee. The French cook."

"Don't joke about this Sidonie, okay?"

"I'm not. It's just that I've always done it, and it's become a habit, I guess."

She looks up at me and smiles the faintest smile. Then her face goes all crooked, and I can tell she's going to bawl. Her face always did that when we were kids just before she really let loose.

"Oh, God, Bobbi," I say, and I drag her into my arms.

She sobs against me. Big choking sobs. "I broke her heart," she says. "That's why she died."

"She died because she was sick, Bobbi."

"But I was so mean to her." She pulls away, her eyes all blotchy. She whips a Kleenex out of its box on her bedside table and blows into it. "It was all the stress and strain of having me be such a total bitch all the time that finally finished her off."

"That isn't true, Bobbi. It isn't easy living with somebody who is sick all the time. It wasn't our fault. It wasn't anybody's fault."

She puts down her Kleenex. "But we could have *been* there. Doesn't that just kill you?"

127

I don't answer her. I don't want to think about it. I don't want to think about Mom dying all alone.

"God," Bobbi sighs. "Sometimes I don't even know what to do anymore. Everything seems so futile. Do you feel that way sometimes?"

"Practically always."

She reaches over and gives me an enormous squeeze. "I love you," she says, "I really do."

I burst into tears. "I love you, too." I sob. "Oh, God, it's my birthday, Bobbi. This is so lousy."

She rubs the tears off my cheek. She kisses it. "I didn't forget," she says.

I smile through my tears. "You didn't?"

She blows her nose again. "Look in my bottom drawer."

I slide off the edge of her bed.

"Right-hand bottom," she says. "I'm sorry that I didn't get a chance to wrap it yet."

I open her dresser drawer. On top of all her neatly folded angora sweaters there's a brown paper bag with Carrie's Ladies Wear written on the front in big green letters.

"Bought it for you last week at Crystal Lake. Phil went with me. He wanted to buy you a pink one with ruffles on it, but I told him I thought it was time you had something more sophisticated. And since you seem to like mine so much, well . . ." She's crying again.

I pull out a sleek black bathing suit with the tiny Jantzen diver stitched low on the hip. It's almost identical to hers except for a little different detailing on the front.

"Roberta — it's beautiful. Thank you. Oh, I love it."

"I'm glad," she says with a huge sob. "Happy birthday. I hope you enjoy wearing it."

128

"Oh, I will. I will. This is the best present. This is going to look so good on me. My God, I'll look like a movie star." I hold it up against me, looking at myself in Bobbi's long dresser mirror.

"It's from both Phil and me. He paid for half of it. He wanted you to have something from him, too."

I turn away from the mirror. She looks very small in her bed.

"Do you love him, Bobbi?"

"I don't know." She collapses forward, her head between her blanketed knees. "Yes, I do know," throwing her head back again, looking at the ceiling. "I love him — I love him so much." She sinks back in bed and pulls her sheet up around her chin. "I just want to *die*. Why doesn't he call? I thought he felt the same way. What's wrong with me, Sidonie?"

"Nothing's wrong with you."

"Then why won't he call?"

"Does he know you feel the same way?"

"Why wouldn't he? On Saturday night, he was the one who made us stop. He was the one who had to say, 'Let's cool down.' And after we'd smoked about four cigarettes, he played with my hair and bet me twenty dollars that I couldn't quit, and I said that he had to quit, too. Then he kissed me for a long time. I said, 'Don't go yet,' and he said, 'Bobbi, you're driving me crazy. I'll call you tomorrow.' But he didn't. I've been waiting ever since."

"Maybe you should call him."

"What would I say?"

"I don't know. Tell him how you feel?"

"Oh, God, I'm so mad. I'm an intelligent person. I'm

129

going to be a doctor. Why is he treating me like I'm just some cheap thrill" — she rubs her tears off on the edge of her sheet — "when all I want to do is love him. Why is he treating me like this?"

"I honestly don't know."

"Will you let me sleep?"

"I'll go. But Bobbi?"

"Yes?"

"Are you sleeping a lot, lately? Or just lying there?"

"A bit of both. I keep thinking about Mom, and Phil, and my miserable life. I've got so much to think about I can't get to sleep. And then when I do sleep, I wake up feeling like I've been run over by a truck. I can hardly move."

"I know the feeling."

"You do?"

"Yes. I think it's okay, Bobbi."

She starts to cry again, very softly. Her blanket is like another skin; it quivers up and sinks down with each wave of sadness.

"Bobbi," I say as I start to leave her room, "I don't know if this is true or not. But when guys and girls fall in love, well, maybe the guys just go around acting a little weird for a while. You know, until they get used to the idea? Did you ever think of that?"

"I don't know," she says, between little breaking sobs. "Just close the door, please. Okay?"

23 ⟶◉⟶

There's a sign about to wobble over and fall off the McMorrans' porch steps. It looks as if it were put there in a big hurry. Written in black block letters, the message says: ARE WE STILL FRIENDS? It wasn't there half an hour ago, before I went in and woke up Roberta.

I pick up the receiver, call him, and he answers immediately, as if he's been pacing around with his phone in his hand.

"It's me," I say.

"I know." There's a silence, nothing but air. Then he says, "Can I see you?"

"Yes," I say calmly. "If you want to."

"I want to. Can we go to the beach?"

"That would be fine. I'll meet you outside in a few minutes."

I hang up the phone. I'm not quite ready to forgive him, but I race upstairs and whip my new bathing suit out of its bag. I stumble around trying to pull it on while at the same time dragging an old raggedy pair of pedal pushers out of my dresser drawer. My hands are shaking so badly that I have to apply lipstick twice, removing it in between times with the cuff of a sock that got tangled up with some other stuff on my dressing table. Then I pull on a bleached-out sleeveless blouse and go slowly out to meet him.

He's standing in the middle of the street. He watches as I saunter toward him.

"You look pretty," he says when I'm right under his chin. Hand under my arm, he steers me off toward the lake. He looks straight ahead and says, "I missed you."

The first thing he wants to do when we get to the beach is to have a look inside the boathouse, which is actually a fifty-year-old converted one-room schoolhouse, now roofed with tar paper. It takes me a while to remember the lock combination, and the lock itself is a tad rusty, but we finally get the door open. The windows are boarded over, and the morning sunlight spills through the open door onto the dry-docked boats — a dilapidated canoe, a rotting, paint-blistered dinghy, and the sailboat.

"It's probably a bit leaky," I say as Kieran trails one hand along the dusty side of the sailboat. "Dad used to patch it up every spring."

"Can't you take it out on the lake anymore?"

"I don't think it would be safe. Dad used to take us all out, right up until the summer before Mom died. He hasn't bothered with it now for two years. I guess it reminds him too much of the fact that he built it for her."

Kieran says, "That week my dad and I went sailing at

132

Rice Lake? He bought the boat, he said, for just him and me. He told me there'd be lots of summers for sailing."

We walk across the gray leaf-littered floor and out into the glare of the hot sun.

I jump off the dock. On the beach, I pull off my pedal pushers and top. I casually stand around in my new bathing suit.

Nothing stirs in the already sweltering heat. There's hardly a breath of wind. The water right along the shore is a hot soupy green. High up the steep wooded hill, in an almost direct line behind the table rock, a cicada's shrill, high call, like the buzzing of a miniature saw, breaks out into the quiet.

I look back. Kieran's now sitting at the far end of the dock. His fountain pen has appeared from nowhere. He's drawing a muddy blue ink blotch on the skin between his thumb and forefinger.

"That's a very beautiful pen." I wade back through the water. Alongside the dock, I turn and hoist myself up beside him.

He probably thinks my new bathing suit is the same one I usually wear. Maybe he doesn't know that one is Roberta's — or maybe he thinks we own identical suits. Which of course we do now, more or less. But I love this suit anyway, even if he won't look at me in it. I love the way it feels so slippery and silky on my body.

"Somebody gave this pen to me," Kieran says. Capping it, he shoves it into the back pocket of his rolled-up chinos. He dangles his feet in the water.

The cicada calls from another, closer, tree. I've never

actually seen one of these insects, but you can't miss their sawing whine.

"It's from my dad." Kieran licks the thumb on his other hand and smears the ink blotch.

Moving closer to him, I say, "It looks expensive."

"It was. Very. And he made sure that I knew it. Kind of a going-away gift, I guess you'd call it." His eyes dart toward the sound of the cicada. "A guilt gift."

He slowly drags his hand through the water, then pulls it, blue-skinned, out again.

I take his hand, and so that he won't think I'm trying to hold it, I start to rub it against mine making some of the blue from his father's gift transfer onto my skin.

He makes me stop by holding my hand. "What's that sound?" he asks.

"It's coming from a bug. He's calling for his mate."

"Dangerous-sounding bug," says Kieran, tightening his grip. "What does he do if she answers?"

I try to pull away. He won't let go. I pull harder. We're eye to eye. His face is tight. His eyes are angry. It's as if we're in some contest about who is the strongest, and it starts to scare me.

"Kieran, just stop it," I say in a firm, cold voice.

The burning sun reflects off the water. The cicada shrills again. Kieran relaxes his grip, but he still won't let go.

"What is *wrong* with you?"

Staring back into the water, he lifts my hand and softly kisses the skin where the blue has rubbed off. He places it carefully in my lap. With a heavy sigh, he lies back on the dock.

134

"Why did you do that?" I demand, looking down at him.

He turns his face away.

"I'm going for a swim," I say, making an effort at sounding calm. "And you should, too, if it'll put you in a better mood."

I ease away from the rough wood planks and slip into the lake. This close to shore, the surface water is hot. I move backwards, a little farther out to where there is a cooler part.

Kieran gets up and peels down to his swimming trunks. He splashes headfirst past me. He swims out a long way. I watch as he turns around and swiftly swims back.

He stands right up beside me and avoids my eyes. "Want to learn how to swim?" he asks, looking up into the trees.

"I hate being facedown," I say angrily. "It scares me, and I don't enjoy being scared." I raise my eyes to his.

"I'm sorry," he says, watching me steadily as he takes my hand again.

I pull it away and hide it under the water.

"Okay?" He slowly reaches down, still watching me.

I let him raise my hand. He places it, palm down, on the surface of the water. He stretches out my fingers. He places his own hand under the water, gently lifting my palm with the very tips of his fingers.

"It's dangerous to live close to a lake," he says, looking at my hand, "and not know how to swim. I'll teach you the sidestroke. Just think of it as kind of a relaxed sideways dog paddle. It's easy. Just the side of your head goes in the water — that's all."

135

"As long as we stay close to shore," I say. "I'm not going anywhere near out there."

"We don't have to."

We do stay close to shore. He swims, demonstrating arm movements, leg kicks, right along beside me. Sometimes, just as I'm starting to feel panicky, I'll feel his leg nudge up against mine, or his hand slip up along my back. On my side I almost stop thinking about what's in the deep deep water.

And he's right — it's easy. For me anyway, it's the easiest way to swim.

After a while we come out of the water. We spread towels on the shale and sprawl out in the sun.

I turn my head and say, "If your mom decides to stay, instead of going back to work in Toronto, then I might get to be a fairly good swimmer."

I want him to tell me that he'll call up Lenore Hoogstraten and break up with her; that he doesn't want to go back to live in Toronto, that he wants to stay here with me.

He folds his arms under his head and watches immense banks of sugar-colored clouds overhead. Smaller gauzy puffs drift past those into comic-book blue. "When I get married," he says, "that'll be it. Did your mom and dad ever fight?"

"They argued sometimes. Everybody does."

"Yeah. I guess that's true." He props his head on his elbow. "Do you read *Mad* magazine?"

"Doesn't everybody?" I look for a small cloud. Find one. From here, it's the size of a dime. I wonder if I could concentrate hard enough to make it evaporate.

"They did a takeoff on 'Santa Claus Is Coming to Town.' It's about drunks. They called it 'Sodden Clods Are Painting the Town.' It was pretty funny," he says without a smile. "Drunks screaming and yelling all over the place. Smashing things up."

I look back at the cloud. It's still there. I don't know why he's telling me all this, and I don't think I want to know. "I saw that," I say.

"Yeah? You read that here while I was reading it in Toronto. We didn't even know each other then." He turns his gaze back up to the sky.

If that cloud disappears by the time we leave this beach, that will mean that Kieran loves me. And then something will happen — I don't know what, but some unexpected thing that will make it so that he doesn't have to go back to Toronto. I close my eyes, tight, and then I roll over on my side.

He turns over on his side, too, head on his elbow again, facing me, and says, "How did they meet?"

"Who?"

"Your mom and dad."

"By chance."

"Yeah?" He reaches out his finger and traces a line down my collarbone. "Tell me."

"He was a starving, in-debt, newly graduated doctor," I say, "and he had a dream one night that he'd placed a bet on a horse named Blue Midnight. And that it came in first in a big race and won him a lot of money."

The same old colors and sounds come rushing in, like a spring day through a door somebody's forgotten to close.

When Bobbi and I were younger we never got tired of hearing Mom's story about how they met. To us, it was the ultimate.

"Go on," says Kieran. He's started to play with my fingers, and I don't even think he's thinking about the fact that he's doing it.

"He woke up in the morning and looked in the newspaper for an afternoon race with any entry that had the words 'midnight' or 'blue.' A horse named Lucky Blue Lady was running in the third race. He got dressed and went down to the track and placed a week's grocery money to win."

"And it won."

"Lucky Blue Lady trailed in fifth. Dad lost all his money. On the tram going home, he saw Mom for the first time. She was wearing a blue dress and a matching hat. She loved to tell this story, especially when Dad was around. She'd say, 'It was one of those silly little hats with the veil that came down over the eyes, and your dad told me later, "Even through that veil I could tell you were the one for me, and I knew my lucky day had finally come."'"

In the sun, Kieran's heart beats against his skin. I rest my head back on the towel. He looks down at me, still tangling my fingers with his. The pupils of his eyes are large and deep and black. I close my eyes, waiting.

He moves beside me, hand dropping my hand, knee grazing my thigh. The sun over the lake lights up my closed eyelids. I hear a splash in the water, and the sun beats down on my mouth, my chin, my body, and I hear the thrashing of his arms and legs as he steadily swims away.

138

I open my eyes. I trace a line from one sugar-loaf cloud to another. I let my eyes wander toward the dime-size cloud. There it is. It's just moved over a couple of feet. I'm going to have to concentrate a lot harder to make it disappear.

24 ──❦──

On Sunday morning, just as if he's never been away, Phil shows up around nine-thirty, hair shining, shoes shining, suit pressed, white shirt, brown tie with a diamond pattern, argyle socks.

"Don't you look spiffy," I say with no enthusiasm.

I don't know whether to hug him or hit him. Last night Bobbi wouldn't come down for supper so I made her a fried egg sandwich with lots of ketchup — just the way she likes it — and then I took it up and stayed with her in her room until she ate it all.

"Roberta home?" He looks around the kitchen where I am standing, barefoot, wrapped in Mom's old quilted blue dressing gown, waiting for Dad to finish dressing so I can give him grapefruit and poached eggs on toast.

"Depends," I say, biting into my own cold toast.

He suddenly grabs my head between both hands and smacks his lips to my forehead. "She's still in bed, right?"

Unshaven, Dad saunters into the kitchen. His eyes widen. "Going somewhere?" he says, surveying under bushy eyebrows Phil's Sunday clothes.

"I'm taking your daughter to church — if that's all right, sir." Phil now has me in a friendly headlock.

"Which daughter?" my father responds.

"Bobbi isn't going anywhere," I say, squirming around.

He releases me. "She's in bed, right?" He looks miserable and optimistic at the same time.

Dad morosely pokes at the eggs in the warming oven. "Has hardly left it for a week. You're welcome to her. The rest of us have totally failed to make her into a responsible human being. We're all going to the dogs around here."

"I beg your pardon," I say. "Who made your breakfast?"

I follow Phil into the front hall. "What the heck is up?"

"What do you mean?"

"I thought you were an atheist. And where on earth have you been for this whole entire week?"

"Working. A lot." He lifts one foot, puts it on the stair landing, examines his brown and red wool sock. "I phoned my brother. Told him that Bobbi's responsible for . . . bringing me back into the church."

"Since when?"

"Today . . . maybe." With the edge of his thumb, he rubs the banister. "George thinks we've been to church every Sunday for the past two months. 'I'd like to meet this young woman' were his actual words." Eyes on the banister, he continues, "She's mad at me, right?"

"Yes, she is. And so am I. You come waltzing in here like everything's supposed to be peachy keen because you've

141

finally shown up. Well, it isn't. Bobbi's in love with you, and she's in a very bad state of mind."

"Aha." He nods his head wisely but isn't moving. "So, she's still talking to me — right?"

"Maybe."

Phil rockets up the stairs, taking two at a time.

"Wait a minute," I call as he disappears around the first landing. "I still want to talk to you."

He pops his head around the corner, comes down again, and sits on the narrow landing. I squeeze in beside him.

"Shoot," he says.

"I want to thank you for my beautiful birthday present."

"You're welcome," he says, pulling at his shoe ties.

"I also want to tell you that if you hurt my sister, I'll kill you."

"Fair enough."

"I mean it."

He sighs, sits back, pulls at his chin, and taps his shoe on the stair. "Your sister," he says, "scares the hell out of me." He turns and gives me a pained, embarrassed smile. "I needed some time to think. You're too young to know about these things."

This is the man who would have chosen for me the pink swimsuit with the ruffles. "So — you now believe in the religious concept of heaven?"

"I'm going to believe in Roberta first," he says, smiling like I'm a little kid. "Maybe heaven will come later. How's that?"

"I'm serious, Phil."

"I'm sorry. I've upset you," he says, and gives me a quick hug.

142

"Don't tell me what I'm feeling. And don't treat me like some two-year-old who doesn't have a brain. I'm sixteen."

"Right," he says agreeably.

"Bobbi is supposed to be the one with all her marbles intact. And I don't understand you at all. What did you do? Call your brother to ask his permission to see her?"

"Something like that. It's very complicated."

"It's very weird, Phil."

"Look, I owe him a lot. He's an old-fashioned Chinese guy."

"You owe Bobbi an explanation. She's having an old-fashioned nervous breakdown. She's never acted like this before, and I don't know what to do about it."

Phil gets to his feet. He hurries up the stairs to Bobbi's bedroom.

I slowly get up off the stair and walk down to the dining room, where Dad sits, pouring pepper all over the eggs I cooked for him.

The only person I've ever known who cooked eggs better than me was Auntie Monique. But then, she's the real French chef of the family. From the middle drawer in the dining room buffet I wriggle out the family photo album. I turn around and put it on the dining room table. I flip open the album to the first page and slide it up to Dad's veined, freckled forearm.

There's a black-and-white photo of Mom and Monique and Lucille in summer dresses. Standing together, arms entwined, they are caught forever in the back garden of their house in Montreal as they mug for some unknown

143

person behind the camera. Mom's not much older than Bobbi. Monique's around twenty-four. Lucille, the baby, is probably seventeen. Their hair is identically styled — waved at the front (Lucille's is the waviest) and pulled back into low buns. They have the same smiles; you can tell they're sisters. Auntie Lucille, however, isn't the beauty of the family. It's clear as day that Mom is.

"The last time we saw Monique was at the funeral," says Dad, cutting into his eggs.

He always calls it the funeral. Never your mother's funeral or Eugenie's funeral.

He continues with a flat expression, "Monique was upset because it wasn't a Catholic cemetery."

"She'll have gotten over it."

He shoots me a look. "Lucille never quite got over me marrying your mother. It was something your mother and I never discussed, but Lucille had . . . you know. A kind of crush on me."

"She'll have gotten over it."

A small chuckle wells up from his throat. He has this wide-eyed expression as if I've just surprised him speechless.

I press on. "It's time that Auntie Monique and Auntie Lucille came for a visit."

"I really appreciate this special effort you've taken with my breakfast," Dad says, looking at my perfectly shaped, perfectly cooked eggs as though they're little balls of canned cat food.

"Call her."

"Who?"

144

"You know perfectly well who. Auntie Monique. And get her to convince Lucille. Say you'll pay for the plane ticket from Cincinatti. Say it's time we had a family reunion."

"I can't do that, Sidonie."

"Why not?"

"You just can't call people up like that. When you haven't seen them for a long time."

"The last time I saw Auntie Monique, she was crying over her sister's grave. The time before that, they were laughing and crying *together* in Monique's kitchen. Don't you remember? I had my eighth birthday there?" I'm grasping at air now, for anything. I look at his eggs and rush on. "Ice cream balls. Auntie Monique's saskatoon pie was so hot from the oven, they made puddles in the middle of the wedges she cut for Mom and Bobbi and me. I want the aunts to come. It's what I want for my birthday, which you forgot."

Flash of brilliance. I wait for all this to sink in.

His face registers extreme pain. He lays down his napkin. Sits back in his chair as if he's just been shot. "It was yesterday, wasn't it?"

"I'll live," I say, picking up his spoon, helping myself to his peppery eggs. "Especially now that you've got this fabulous opportunity to redeem yourself."

He mutters, "I'm so sorry," then something else I can't hear. I'm afraid to look at him. Maybe I don't want to see him cry after all. In fact, at this moment I can't think of anything I'd rather see less.

He gets up from the table and goes out to the kitchen. I

145

hear him go through the fridge. He's pretending that I forgot to get him something. He then spends about five minutes aimlessly opening and closing drawers and cupboards. Overhead, I hear Roberta's muffled voice, then Phil's. Dad finally comes back with a glass of milk.

He hates milk. I hate milk. He sets it down in front of me. I look up. He's been crying. His eyes are red. He says, clearing his throat, "Would you like some chocolate Nestle's Quik with that?"

"Yes," I say. "That would be really nice, Dad."

He goes back out to the kitchen.

Bobbi and Phil appear in the archway between the living and dining rooms. His hands are in his pockets. Her eyes are puffy, and little red dots, from hard crying, are sprinkled across her nose and cheeks.

"We're going to church." Bobbi picks up the end of one of the ties on her dressing gown. She begins to fold it up into a neat roll. She looks back at Phil. "I'll get dressed. Do you want some breakfast?"

"No thanks," he says with a handsome smile. He reaches out his thumb and runs it across her bottom lip.

She pulls back, and two angry lines appear between her eyebrows. "Don't," she says. "Just don't."

Phil drops his hand as if it's been burned.

Dad appears from the kitchen with a spoon and the Quik. With sharp little looks at each of them, he spoons chocolate powder into my milk, stirs it. Some milk and tiny brown clumps wash over the side. He keeps stirring. The milk slowly turns to light beige. I watch, with growing interest, as it continues to wash over and puddle onto the tablecloth.

146

"It's time this family started to get back to normal," Dad says. "Roberta, your sister has asked if I will call up both Monique and Lucille and ask if they would consider paying us a visit. I have decided that that is what I'm going to do."

25 ⟶⊘⟵

One hour in church on Sunday has turned Roberta back into a shrew. During the past three days, she's gone back to her summer job and, as well, our house fairly gleams. She has scrubbed and waxed all the floors on her hands and knees and has begun to redecorate the guest room with stunning dark rose wallpaper.

The aunts are coming for four days, starting Friday evening. My idea. She's acting as if it were hers.

It was Lucille, up from the States for a visit, who answered when Dad called Monique's house. She was so surprised and speechless, he said, that she immediately handed over the phone to Monique, who said, "What? Of course we'll come. We'd love to!"

"Easy as pie," said Dad when he got off the phone. He looked pretty surprised himself. Then all at once he said, thunderstruck, "What on earth are we going to do with these women?"

"We'll entertain them," I said, lifting his plate from the table and walking with it out to the kitchen.

On Wednesday morning I tell Bobbi that I'm planning the aunts' welcome-back-to-the-family dinner. She smoothes the top corner of the wallpaper strip she's just finished hanging and says, paste dripping down her arms, "But you can't cook."

"I can so cook. You just never let me."

There's a white blob of paste stuck in her hair. Queen-like, she pushes past me out into the upstairs hall.

"I want to know if Kieran and I can have the car tomorrow," I say, following her into the bathroom. "He has his driver's license, and there are some things that I'll need to buy for the dinner."

She flips on the taps and scrubs her hands and arms. The water turns white and sails down the sink. "I can't let you have the car." She turns off the taps, goes to the lime green towel by the sink.

"Why not?"

"I have the meal all arranged," she says, "but if you're going to do it, go ahead. But you are not having the car. I'm sorry — that's just the way it is." She struts off, huffing and snorting, her nose plastered to the ceiling.

Phil's back in her life, practically standing on his head to accommodate her moods, and I have arranged a much-needed family get-together. I don't know what more she wants.

Good Housekeeping, Betty Crocker, and a few other books are my guides on Wednesday and Thursday.

"Hilda's Ham and Endives Au Gratin," Kieran reads aloud. "What the heck's a Belgian endive?"

149

"Beats me," I say, shoving a peanut-butter cookie into my mouth. We're sitting at the kitchen table.

"Well" — he shuts the book — "I'm going for another swim."

All week he's been going for "another swim" a lot. For the first while, he said he didn't want me coming along because he's "training" and has to be alone when he trains. Now that I need to be at home getting ready for the aunts' visit, he simply ups and goes. He spends less and less time with me and more and more time at the lake, working off whatever it is that's bugging him.

"Crumbs." He flicks a piece of cookie off the side of my mouth.

I bite my tongue. Actually bite it. I sit, in pain, holding my hand over my mouth.

"Sidonie," he says, appalled, his hand on my wrist, "one of these days you're going to kill yourself."

I rush to the sink. I stick my head under the tap and rinse out the blood. I come up from the cold running water and he's gone again.

I continue working until I've finished all the baking for the aunts' visit: two dozen peanut-butter cookies, two dozen chocolate chip cookies, a coffee marshmallow refrigerator cake, double-decker brownies, and lemon bars. All these I've made with whatever I could find — clumped-up cocoa, old lemons, rock-hard marshmallows. There were no fresh chocolate chips. Just a bag of gray ones. Everything cooked up looking and smelling good, no thanks to Roberta.

Kieran breezes into the kitchen four hours after he left,

looking cool and clean and relaxed. I slide the last batch of cookies from the 400-degree oven.

He looks at my work spread all over the counters. "All this trouble you're going to," he says. "The only other person I've seen go to this much work for guests is Mrs. Hoogstraten. Every year she bakes a whole bunch of stuff for their New Year's Day party."

He follows me from the stove to the table, where I start to lift off the cookies to cool them on wire racks. "When she goes to get the rum balls," he continues, "at least half of them are missing. She always hides them, and Mike and Lenore and I always find them. They're great after a swim meet. Lenore joined the same swim club that Mike and I have belonged to since we were about eight. She's only been at it a couple of years, but she won a bronze in Minneapolis this spring. She's a strong swimmer."

"Oh, really," I say, gagging down another cookie. "She must be very slim. All that exercise."

He doesn't even twig to the fact that I'm being sarcastic. Picks up three chocolate chip cookies. Eats them. Goes for a fourth. "These are fantastic. My mother," he says, "*if* she ever gets around to baking, always burns everything. Dad used to blow his top. We ate out — a lot. Lately, though, she's starting to cook a little more for just us two. She's actually quite a good cook — when she's cooking stuff that I like. She even sings old Russian songs. It's pretty interesting."

I don't really care to hear about the sacred Toronto Hoogstratens or his parents' weird awful marriage after he's just disappeared on me for four entire hours.

151

When Roberta gets home, I ask him to stay for supper. He says he's not sure if he can or not. He must catch my I-want-to-kill-you look, because he goes into the living room to call his mom.

I say, trying one more time, "Bobbi, I don't understand why Kieran and I can't have the car just to go and get a few groceries."

"The subject is closed," she says, hauling a head of lettuce out of the fridge.

"So when will I get the groceries?"

"I have no idea."

"Bitch," I mutter under my breath.

"I beg your pardon?"

"Want me to spell it?"

"That won't be necessary," she says coldly. "Get out of my kitchen."

"I will," I say. "You want to do everything yourself? Fine. There's a dirty floor. There's the pile of cookie tins I didn't put away. And look — there's crusty egg oozing down one side of the stove. And a sink full of dishes just waiting for you to play Cinderella over. Enjoy yourself."

I leave the kitchen. Behind me, the fridge door is slammed violently shut. A small booming sound rolls off the metal sides.

In the living room, Phil has started up his Jerry Lee Lewis imitation, playing and singing "Great Balls of Fire." Kieran beats out time with his hands on top of the piano, down the sides of the piano, along the front of the piano. He bobs his head up and down.

I walk over to the sofa and fall into it. I watch them grin at each other like a couple of maniacs. They're having a

152

good time. Maybe they'll become friends. Maybe Kieran will get a new set of drums. They could play together and have the beginnings of their own jazz combo. By then, Phil and Roberta and Kieran and I would all be in the city, working or going to university. We'd hop the bus home on the weekends (or maybe by then Phil would have his own car). We'd visit Dad, who'd be so glad to see us he'd take the entire weekend off from work just to be around for small chats and meals together.

This is just a fantasy. I know that. Bobbi and Phil will likely break up. Kieran will take a plane back to Toronto, and I'll never see or hear from him again. We'll all go our separate ways. I'll be as lonely as ever.

I can tell that Phil is impressed with Kieran's piano drumming. He launches into "Fascinating Rhythm," and he doesn't play it as fast as he usually does. He doesn't make a big deal of this, just loosens up his shoulders and glides his strong fingers along the keys at a relaxed pace. I know he's doing this to give Kieran a chance. The rhythm isn't easy. The way Phil plays it, it just sounds easy.

A quarter of the way in, Kieran gives up. He comes away from the piano. "It's useless without my drums," he says, plopping down on the sofa, just missing my feet.

Phil thunders down the keys. He swings his legs up over and around the piano bench. "You must play them pretty well," he says, bending forward with interest.

"Yeah, I guess," Kieran replies. He turns his head around to watch the sun sinking down the sky. He drums his fingers on the back of the sofa.

Pots are being banged around in the kitchen. The drawer under the stove is suddenly shoved, clanging, shut.

Phil and I stare at each other. Roberta is working herself up into a thoroughly shrewish mood.

Phil flares his nostrils, crosses his eyes, puts an imaginary gun to his head, and pulls the trigger. Then he falls over sideways on the piano bench. I burst into giggles.

Kieran comes and stands beside me. "I need some fresh air."

I sink to the floor, holding my stomach, while Phil kicks his legs and makes gagging sounds.

"What is this — Laurel and Hardy?" says Kieran. "Are you coming with me, or aren't you?"

"Yes," I say, catching my breath. "Just wait, okay?"

He stands there looking at me, then looking at Phil — as if we're conspirators in some kind of plot to do him in.

"I said" — he suddenly reaches down, grabs my arm, and roughly starts to pull me to my feet — "I want you to come with me."

Startled, I lose my balance. I topple back onto the carpet just as Bobbi shows up from the kitchen. Pulling off her apron, she throws it at Phil. He catches it, sits up, looks at it crumpled in his hands.

Bobbi turns and slumps against the living room wall. He drops the apron. "What's up?" he says, getting to his feet.

Kieran slowly sinks down beside me, watching them.

Bobbi shakes her head and rolls away from Phil and then hides around the corner in the hallway. I can see the tips of her red nail-polished toenails. Phil darts around the corner, pulling her with him completely out of sight. She's crying softly, and he's whispering, "What's wrong?"

It's quiet for a while. Finally, Bobbi's angry choked

154

voice, "Damn it, I'm sick of everything. I'm sick of this goddamn house. I'm sick of nobody ever asking me what I think or how I feel. I'm just expected to be this — this *person* who's always here. Always doing everything all by myself. I can't stand it anymore!"

More silence. "Let's go to Crystal Lake." Phil's voice. "I'll buy you dinner. We'll talk. Okay? Come on, Bobbi. Don't you know it doesn't have to be this way? Oh, come here, you're breaking my heart."

Silence. More whispers. Then they go into the kitchen. And then out the screen door. It squeaks, then thuds shut.

In a couple of minutes, the car starts up and drives away. The gravel crunches and pings under the tires.

Kieran and I still sit on the living room floor. I get up and go out to the kitchen. He follows me. He opens the fridge for a chunk of ham and I slide my head under his arm to get the mayonnaise and a couple of bottles of Coke. Shoulder to shoulder, we make our sandwiches. We sit very close at the kitchen table to eat them. Each time I set my hand down, his is right there beside it.

After dinner, he scrapes off our plates. He puts hot sudsy water in the sink and washes all the dishes. I dry them. He wipes down the counter and cleans the dried egg off the stove, and I sweep the floor. He stacks my cookie tins neatly in the refrigerator.

Then we go back to the living room and sit, and he ever so gently circles his arm along the back of the sofa so that the back of my head almost touches his arm, and we watch *77 Sunset Strip* and a few other shows until sign-off time at eleven o'clock.

When my father comes home, he doesn't even notice us

at the end of the darkened hallway, in the front vestibule, not touching, saying, "See you," and "Okay, tomorrow," as the misty half-moon peeks over the trees beyond the window at the top of the door.

I watch Kieran lope off home, between the fir trees, across the street. He does a little dance up his porch steps. He turns and waves. I wave back and slowly close the door.

In the kitchen, Dad's lifting a thin round slice of ham off the breadboard.

"Dad," I say, "I need the car tomorrow morning because I'm making dinner for Auntie Monique and Auntie Lucille and I have to buy some things. And I'll need this week's grocery money, so please don't give it to Bobbi."

He pops the ham into his mouth. Wipes his fingers on his pants and smiles at me. "When did you get your license?"

"I didn't. I don't know how to drive. So far, nobody's offered to teach me."

"I taught your sister."

"I know."

"How do you propose to drive the car?"

"Kieran will drive it."

"Who?"

"Dr. McMorran's son."

"Oh. Yes. Pretty good driver, is he?"

"I don't know. He has his license."

"Ah. Well, then . . . I suppose that would be all right. But leave the driving lessons up to me. Agreed?"

"Okay."

He says, looking at me closely, "Next week, I'll start trying to get home a little earlier."

156

"I won't hold my breath."

"There are two bottles of Chateau Margaux in the cellar," he says, ignoring this, with a mild sniff and a glance at the ceiling. "A splendid red wine that your mother and I were saving for a special occasion. I think they would go nicely with this dinner of yours, so you can serve them if you like. Why aren't you going grocery shopping with your sister?"

"She doesn't think I can handle this dinner. She wanted to do it all herself. And she's not acting like a normal person. She's worse then ever."

"I know."

"I wish she'd snap out of it."

"She will."

"How do you know?"

"She's in love."

"How do *you* know?"

He gives me a tired wrinkled freckled smile and leans over, kissing my forehead. "Good night, Muffet," he says. "I'll leave the money on my dresser, and I'll have a little talk with Bobbi when I see her on the wards tomorrow. Turn out the lights before you come up to bed."

"Dad?"

"Yes?"

"Are you glad about the aunts' visit?"

"Glad?" He cocks his head, as if he's thinking about it — about the actual feeling of glad. Then he says, "Yes," and nods at his feet. "Yes," he says again in a louder voice. "I *am* glad. It will liven up this old place."

Roberta Anne Fallows does not appear until five o'clock

in the morning, when the birds are twittering like crazy and the sun is rising red and Dad is sawing off logs in his room. Sandals swinging in her hands, she comes sneaking up the stairs into the darkness of the upstairs hall. My bedroom door is open, my pillows adjusted so I can get a good bead on her. It's still quite dark as she slips, quiet as a lullaby, into her bedroom.

26 ⟿

Three hours later, Kieran appears at the screen door. He slides into the kitchen and takes the milk out of the refrigerator and pours himself a glass. "You okay?" he says in a low voice.

I whisper back, "No change since I called you ten minutes ago. How about you?"

"I'm okay. Couldn't sleep, though. I was awake all night."

Bogie, blinking and ecstatically purring, waits patiently by my feet. I throw some cheese onto the floor for him.

Kieran comes over and stands right by my elbow, leaning his long body against the counter, drinking his milk.

"So Bobbi got in late."

"Late, late, late," I say. He smells very good. His warm arm prickles against mine.

"You never said how late." He drums his fingers on his milk glass.

"Five in the morning late."

"Ah," he says, and polishes off his milk. "That's late."

Roberta wanders into the kitchen on her way to work.

"Hi, Bobbi," Kieran says in a loud friendly manner. "How are you this morning?"

"I'm fine." Red flushes up her throat. "How else should I be?"

"Did you sleep well?" I ask her innocently.

"Very well, thank you, and I'm very very late for work," she says, dashing out of the door with Bogie running and hopping like a fat rabbit behind her.

She appears again, beyond the window screens. The sun slants down her hair as she hurries along. Bogie soon gives up trying to follow. He sits down in the middle of the sidewalk and watches until the fresh green shadows and sunlight have melted her into the morning. A bee zooms near his head. He whips around, leaps into the air, and misses. The bee bounces off the screen and wings away to the roses side of the house.

Kieran says, "So where are the car keys?"

"On the hall table."

"And it's okay."

"Dad said."

"I thought Bobbi runs the show."

"Not always."

He rubs the palms of his hands along the edge of the counter. "I've been thinking," he says slowly, as if he's pulling himself out of a half-dream.

"About what?"

"The way Phil acted with her last night. He's not one of

these guys that order women around. Know what I'm talking about?"

I nod my head. I'm remembering the way Kieran grabbed my arm and demanded that I get up and go outside with him. Then I think of Phil and how he gently pulled Bobbi around the corner of the living room to comfort her. Even though she was angry.

"Neither Phil or your dad are the kind of guys who push their weight around. Dr. Hoogstraten either." Kieran bites away at a hangnail, looks at his finger, rubs it with his thumb. "I mean, they're all just regular guys who try to be good people."

"I know that. What's your point?"

"People" — he pauses and thinks about this — "people don't have to be the way they worry they might turn out to be — do they?" He drops his hand and sort of mumbles, "For instance, like their fathers?"

"No." I remember what Phil said to Bobbi, and I add quietly, "It doesn't have to be that way."

He turns his face. "I'm thinking maybe I should call Lenore Hoogstraten and be honest with her and break up." His eyes are flat. He doesn't want me to see what he's feeling. Maybe he just wants to see what I'm feeling.

I'm beginning to wonder myself. "When will you call her?"

"Tomorrow. Or maybe Monday."

Do I really want to be in love someone who's so mixed up he's worried that he hasn't any control over how he'll turn out? At times, I've been so down in the dumps that I've wondered if I'd ever get out again. But I've never worried that I'd become an alcoholic who went around smashing up my children's drum sets. In my mind, I've always been a university graduate with a pretty nice husband and a few kids and a couple of cats. Something like that. I want my life to get better. Not worse.

"It's your life," I say noncommittally.

"I'm not sure how Mike is going to react to all this," he says, looking away, then back at me. "He's pretty close to his sister."

"It's up to you. Let's go grocery shopping."

27 ⏤◎⏤

I 've chosen to do what looks impressive but is guaranteed not to fail: melon ball cocktail to have before dinner with a relish tray (Cheez Whiz on celery sticks and radish roses), whipped potatoes on the half shell, green beans almondine, rolls (with chilled butter curls), and coq au vin (you cook the chickens for a while in butter, throw on some herbs and red wine, and bake them in the oven for a couple of hours).

By five o'clock the table is set with all of Mom's good china and silver, freshly laundered and ironed linen tablecloth and napkins, and tall yellow candles. Dad and Mom's two bottles of Château Margaux are on the sideboard. Mashed potatoes wait in half shells to be reheated, the green beans are sliced into strips, and the chickens are in the oven. Cooling on the top shelf of the refrigerator are orange and pink melon balls that rest, drowned in ginger ale, in seven crystal dishes.

As soon as we got back with the groceries, Kieran's mom phoned and asked him to come home for a while. I haven't seen him since. All the way over to Crystal Lake, and then all the way back, he was in another one of his moods, knuckles white along the top of the steering wheel, jaw muscles working, scowling at everything — cows, trucks, stores, passersby. I had more important things to think about than trying to jolly him out of it. Things like maybe the dinner will be a huge flop. Maybe the aunts will start a fight with Dad. Or maybe they'll start crying about Mom at the dinner table. I'd hate that. It would ruin everything.

I go up to the bathroom and pour Lilac Time bubble bath into the water. Our white tub stands on four stumpy feet. The round white porcelain plates on the taps read, in black letters, HOT and COLD. Except the cold water comes out the hot water tap and vice versa. It's been that way ever since I can remember. It occurs to me now that they probably could be switched around so that they'd read properly. I don't know why nobody's thought of this. I make a mental note to warn Lucille and Monique about the hazards of taking a bath in our tub. I step in and sink down until the water comes up to my chin. Suddenly, I feel as if I could float away. I don't remember the last time I felt this relaxed. The water makes an echo in this high-ceilinged room when you let it drip off your hands back into the tub.

I listen to the water. To its echoes. I think back to the baths when I was really small, when Mom would hold the washcloth over me and then squeeze the warm water slowly over my head. I was probably only two at the time. But I remember the sound of dripping water and her soft

164

voice. She'd hum, then gently scrub. There was this song in French. Back then she would sing it to me only during my baths.

Years later, after she'd come home from the infirmary, she taught it to me. I remember that we sang it together fairly often and for no particular reason — other than it was our favorite.

> À la claire fontaine
> M'en allant promener
> J'ai trouvé l'eau si belle
> Que je m'y suis baigné
> Il y a longtemps que je t'aime
> Jamais je ne t'oublierai

It must have made her happy, I think, to bathe me.

Another sound intrudes. Voices on the stairs. Bobbi and Phil? The voices have reached the top of the stairs. Women's voices.

"Hello!" somebody calls. My God, the aunts! They weren't supposed to arrive for another hour. Should I call out to them?

I don't get the chance. The bathroom door swings open. Wide open. My aunts, in dresses, hats, high heels, purses, little white gloves, stand in the doorway.

Older graying Monique (who's put on a fair bit of weight) smiles broadly. She wears no makeup. Her skin is as fresh and pink as a baby's. "Sidonie," she chirps. "Was that you singing in French, Sidonie?"

"Yes," I say, clutching a facecloth to my chest.

"We just let ourselves in!" She turns to Lucille. "See?

What do you think people do in the country? I never leave my door locked. That's important, especially in winter, Lucille. You just don't know who might be freezing to death and need to come in to use the phone or make a cup of coffee and get warmed up." She turns, beaming back to me. "You look more and more like your mother. Big eyes. Mouth is that same pretty shape. Don't you think she's turning into a beauty like little Eugenie, Lucille?"

Skinny Lucille, this aunt whom I've never before laid eyes on, nods and nods. A pillbox hat sort of perches on the back of her head, like a small fat bird. Her wavy hair (it *is* like mine) has been colored by a bottle.

I barely whisper, "Your room is the one with the dark rose wallpaper — down the hall."

"*Merci, petit chou,*" says Monique. "You finish your bath, there." She lowers her voice to a whisper, too, as if we're sharing some kind of incredible secret. "And we'll see you later." She and Lucille leave as one; their floral printed skirts swish around behind them.

I sink up to my nose in bubbles.

28 ⟶꩜

M y God," says Roberta minutes later, flying into
the bathroom as I stagger into my underwear,
"have you seen the aunts?" Not waiting for an answer, she
peels off her uniform. Plunges her arm into the bathtub.
Recorks the water, which has started to slowly slurp down
the drain. "They practically attacked me in the hallway,
exclaiming over the room I'd done for them. Kissing both
cheeks — that's very French, isn't it? Hugging me until my
bones practically rattled." She steps into the tub, grabs the
soap, sudses her face, splashes water all over it. She whips a
lime green facecloth off the towel rack and proceeds to
lather it up. "What'd you think of Lucille? Isn't she glam-
orous?"

"I just saw her for a minute." I pull my full-skirted white
sleeveless dress over my head.

Water drips down her freckles. "Your dinner smells
good."

"I'm glad you approve."

She pushes back her soggy bangs. "Look. I know that I've been a little tense lately."

"Lately?"

"Well, for a long time. Sidonie, I've had to handle everything. From way before Mom died. I didn't think about the fact that maybe I could ask for a little help."

"Bobbi, be honest. You wanted to do the dinner all by yourself so the aunts would tell you how terrific you are and what a great cook and what a fabulous person. And you wanted me to just melt into a corner somewhere."

"That's not true at all."

"Yes it is," I say, yanking up the zipper of my dress. It gets stuck halfway. I tug and tug, but it won't budge either up or down.

I have to wait around until Bobbi gets out of the tub, dries herself off, and goes and puts on her own clothes before she'll come back and help me get it unstuck.

She clatters slowly down the stairs in her white high heels. I walk behind her. She's pinned up her hair like Brigitte Bardot. A little pearl bobbles off the chain clasp at the back of her neck.

Kieran is actually in the kitchen. Entertaining the aunts. He's made coffee for them and has cut each a piece of coffee marshmallow refrigerator cake. His smile is embarrassed, and he doesn't know what to do with his hands, which he's tucked, arms folded, under his armpits.

"This is marrr-vellous," says Lucille. She spoons in another mouthful of cake. She's deeply tanned and has changed into a dark navy sheath. Bare back. Expensive perfume. She wears a pearl choker.

168

"Sidonie," says Monique, "your father never mentioned a handsome boyfriend." She winks at Kieran. He partially hides around the side of the refrigerator, near the door.

I notice a diamond ring on Monique's left hand. It looks new. As we stand around and talk, she plays with it. I lean beside her against the kitchen counter and fold my arms. She awkwardly puts down her cup and throws a plump arm around me. Her new weight feels like a pillow. "Do you remember," she says, "that cake I made for your eighth birthday?"

I nod my head, smiling weakly. "It was pink."

"It was heart-shaped, with coconut cream icing," Bobbi elaborates.

Monique beams. "You have a good memory." She squeezes my shoulders.

"How could I forget a cake like that?" says Bobbi. "It was the nicest birthday cake I'd ever seen. You put icing roses on it."

"I did?" Monique laughs and holds me away from her. "Do you remember any roses? I don't remember roses."

"I do," Bobbi says quietly. "You made three. One for each round part and one for the tip. I wrapped one up in waxed paper and brought it home. I saved it until it got too hard to eat. And then I threw it out."

"Mom was an awful cook," I say, looking at Bobbi. "She always had our birthday cakes made up at the bakery in Crystal Lake. They were nice, but nothing like yours."

Lucille nods her head and scrapes the rest of the whipped cream off her plate. She does that a lot — nods her head. She probably just wants to appear agreeable. She's quite pretty. Wears a fair amount of makeup, but she's put it — you can tell — on top of skin that is like Monique's.

I get a memory flash of Mom, in profile, reading on the sofa in the living room as the late afternoon sun dusts her eyelashes and light and shadows dance along her nose and cheeks — skin like her sisters'.

Dad and Phil saunter up the walk past the kitchen windows. When they get inside, everyone starts laughing and talking at once. Lucille awkwardly hugs Dad. He stiffly kisses her cheek as they come together as though a wall has been suddenly shoved between them. I wonder if she still has a crush on him.

She stands back, smiling, blinking brightly, quickly looking around the kitchen at nothing and nobody in particular — not focusing on any of us.

Monique hugs Dad, and their eyes simultaneously mist up.

"How was your trip down here?" he asks.

"Oh, dusty," says Monique, laughing, rummaging around in her purse for a Kleenex. "Lucille likes our back country roads. Isn't that right, little sister?" she teases. "You may never want to go home to Cincinnati."

Lucille gives her a wilted smile.

Roberta introduces Phil as her boyfriend. He blushes and doesn't look the aunts in the eyes when they're shaking hands. Dad claps him on the back. "A fine young man. He'll do well no matter what area of medicine he chooses." Phil looks as if he'd like to die and sink into the basement.

"Oh, a doctor," exclaims Monique, blowing her nose.

"How nice, Roberta." Lucille smiles and nods several times.

170

In front of the refrigerator, with a quick secret move-ment that only I catch, Roberta clasps Phil's hand and pulls it behind her so that now their joined hands are hidden. His eyes soften, but the rest of him stays edgy.

Dad says, "Why don't we all go sit in the living room?" The aunts trail behind him, followed by Roberta and Phil, who are still holding hands.

I open the oven and slide the tray of potatoes under the roasting chickens. I turn on the front burner for the green beans almondine.

"Mom's gone to Toronto for three days," says Kieran, watching me scrape butter into a pan.

"I'm going to have to get this dinner onto the table as fast as I can," I say tensely, dropping the slivered almonds into the butter.

He hovers beside me. "Visiting Dad. I didn't have a clue until I went home this morning." He unbuttons his shirt cuffs, rolls back his sleeves. "Her suitcase was all packed, waiting at the door when I got there. I practically tripped over it. She told me, 'I have to go and see him.' I said, 'Can't you just phone?' 'No,' she said, 'there are things we need to discuss.' I said, 'Okay, but take me with you.'"

The butter splatters all over the place, and I turn down the heat a couple of notches. "Maybe she just wanted to go on her own."

I want to hear what's going on in the living room. Phil's started up at the piano, and I can tell from the way the aunts are carrying on that he's a real hit.

Kieran picks up the dishrag and fiddles with it. Over the sizzling butter and Phil's jazz, he says, "I kept asking to go, but all she said was, 'It's a long drive to the city, and I've got a three o'clock plane to catch.' I told her, 'That's no excuse.' And just before she left she said, 'I'm sorry I waited so late to tell you. I didn't think you'd be so upset.' " He's stretching the dishrag out of shape. "What kind of a stupid lie is that?"

Phil's playing "Honeysuckle Rose." I remember how Dad used to sing that song to Mom — always off-key because of his tin ear. She loved it. Roberta and I were embarrassed by it. All I can think of is how unusual my parents were together. Even though she was sick most of the time, he really did think that the day he met her was his lucky day. They were in love all of the time they had — twenty years — which, in the larger scale of things, is not exactly what you could call a lifetime.

Does Phil know that this was their song, or is it just some crazy fluke that he's playing it?

Dad starts up like a basement canary. (Bobbi used to say, "Will you sing solo?" "Yeah," I'd add, "so low we can hardly hear it.") He sings, " *'When I'm taking trips, to your tasty lips, your confection fairly drips.' "*

One of the aunts, laughing (maybe it's Lucille), and Phil join in: " *'Everybody knows — you're my honeysuckle rose.' "*

Kieran says, "Sidonie, you're not listening to me. She's going to be in Toronto by herself — with *him.* "

"Maybe they can talk things over." I dump the beans in with the almonds. "Maybe things will work out." I want to be with my family, watching them all get along. They're all singing now — even Roberta. I don't want to hear what he wants to tell me. I don't want to know what it is.

"I'm scared," he says, shoulders slumped over, turning the dishrag over and over in his hands.

172

"Kieran, please let's talk about this later, okay?"

I rapidly scrape down the sides of the steaming pan.

He flips the rag into the sink. "That's it. I'm going," he says, heading for the door.

In shock, I follow him. "Stay for dinner, okay? I said we'll talk about this later."

"There won't be any later."

The screen door slams. He turns and looks at me through the wire mesh. His tie is crooked. His white shirt rumpled. The sky behind him, up beyond screen and wooden slats and treetops, has turned a dark orange. Beads of perspiration have started along his hairline.

"Your mother died," he says. "Well, that's too bad. And you and your sister don't get along. Well, tough. But, you know, you're going to be just fine. You'll be just fine, Sidonie. And Bobbi's got Phil, who's the greatest guy in the world. He'll always take care of her. He'll never let her down."

"Kieran, just stay, okay? I want you to stay." I try pushing open the screen door.

But he shoves it closed and slowly turns his back on it. "Listen to them all in there. You have a family. Don't you know how lucky you are?" He begins to inch around again. "Sidonie? Can I tell you something?"

"Yes, tell me — anything." Please don't tell me this.

"The last time my mother and father were together, he punched her through our glass shower door," he says in a soft sickened voice, the side of his face, his lips, brushing the screen, "and there's blood all over the place and he's dragging her out of the bathtub, out through all that glass and she's screaming. She's crying for him to please stop. To

173

please please stop." He turns completely around to face me. "He's real big. I've never dared hit him before, but I did hit him, and when he didn't try to stop me I just kept on hitting him and hitting him and hitting and hitting until he held me. Oh, God, what's he going to do this time?"

He disappears from the other side of the door. The wind opens it slightly, then bangs it shut. The tops of the trees, lining the ravine, thrash around in the sudden gust — reddish orange, bathed in the sky's light. The wind is only a slight relief from the heavy heated air.

The music stops in the living room, and I hear a commotion as windows are shut. I hear somebody run upstairs to make sure that those windows are shut, too.

I am standing in the middle of the kitchen, and the beans are sizzling in the butter, and I know I should turn down the heat before they burn.

The sky quickly darkens, and Roberta comes through the dining room into the kitchen. Pink rises in her cheeks. I don't remember the last time I saw her so happy.

She floats over and slips her arms around my waist. I smell, faintly, Mom's warm flowery perfume — there's still half a bottle left, sitting on her dresser. She kisses both my cheeks, the French way, and smoothes my hair away from my face and says, "This is the happiest thing that's happened to this family since Mom died. I'm so glad you got Dad to ask them to come here."

29 ⟜ⓔ⟝

Dinner passes like a bad dream. I smile and smile
and smile. I tell them that Kieran hadn't planned
on staying and had to go home. Dad says, frowning,
"That's odd," and goes back to carving the coq au vin. I
endure the gushings of my aunts: "What a sweet boy."
"Such a gentleman."

They talk nonstop during the entire meal. Everyone
except me drinks a couple of glasses of wine. The electricity, from the storm, goes on and off. The candle flames
flicker on. Cracks of thunder rattle the windows.

Toward the end of the first course, Lucille, flushed,
announces, "Monique has recently become engaged. To
Art Barker."

There is a rush of congratulations.

Monique lowers her eyes modestly. "He's a farmer," she
says, and begins to fork down her second helping of coq
au vin.

Lucille, a little drunk, says, "He isn't a Catholic," stops for a minute, paralyzed, and adds, nodding frantically, "He's a widower."

Monique laughs loudly, nervously. "He tells me, 'Monique, you're a beautiful woman. I'll build you a big house.'"

Dad laughs. Monique leans over, hand on his arm, and winks. "Poor Lucille has been jilted three times — all by good Catholics."

Dad laughs all the harder.

Lucille says, "Monique, please. He doesn't need to hear all this."

All during dinner she's been openly flirting with him. And while he hasn't been flirting back, he hasn't exactly been discouraging her either. Does she really think that now Mom is dead and out of the way, she can all of a sudden declare open season on him — on *my father?*

Monique carries on, saying, "We need to call a truce — bury the hatchet. Don't you think? We're all growing older. We can't all be Catholics." She gives Dad's arm a parting pat. "And we don't want to die mad."

"Here, here," says Dad, lifting his glass, toasting the aunts. He even winks at Lucille, who blushes. His voice is loud, and he's laughing at everything the aunts say.

"I'll drink to that," says Roberta, leaning across Phil to help herself to a bit more wine.

Phil just sits there smiling like he's a huge buried treasure and Roberta's the one with the map.

I go out to the kitchen, where the coffee percolator is sputtering all over the kitchen counter. I pull the plug, then open the fridge and start to pull out all the desserts. I

176

think about Kieran all alone at his house with the electricity flicking on and off and the trees outside batting around in the wind.

Roberta walks into the kitchen balancing a pile of dirty plates.

"Bobbi," I say, "I have to go see Kieran."

"Now?"

"Yes."

"Can't it wait? We haven't had dessert or anything." She pauses to set down the plates. "What will the aunts think?"

"I have to go. Now."

"Are you coming back soon?"

"I don't know."

She follows me into the hallway, where I pull off my white slip-ons and step into rubber boots.

"What's wrong?"

I make a tent of my raincoat. "I'll tell you later. I swear I will."

She holds open the door. "This is really bad timing," she says, her voice rising as I run into the storm.

Little broken oak twigs, dark green leaves still attached, litter our street. The rain pelts down. A car, headlights beaming, splashes through the puddles on the lake road. The lights are back on all over — dim rooms at the Coateses'; the chandelier shimmering at Donina Stang's — but the McMorrans' house is as dark as the clouds that roll and boil overhead.

I run up the steps onto the porch and bang on the front door. The hall phone, ringing behind the lace curtain, isn't being picked up. I push open the door and call for

Kieran. My answer is an eerie silence, jangled by the telephone. It rings two more times, then quits. I pull off my mud-slimed boots, throwing them down by the door, and run upstairs, all the while calling his name.

The first bedroom I come to, obviously his mother's, contains a double bed covered with a satin bedspread. A small brass clock ticks loudly on an embroidered cloth on her bedside table. Beside it is a black-and-white photo in a round silver frame — a laughing baby of about two with curly hair and wearing knitted overalls. It must be Kieran.

I swing back into the upstairs hallway. Beside his mother's room is a small bathroom. Next to that is an extra bedroom piled up with large unpacked boxes.

Across the hall I find Kieran's practically empty room. His bed covers are partially thrown over a pillow that hangs halfway off the mattress. On his dresser are several crumpled-up bills, a few dimes, some pennies — nothing else. And the clothes he wore over to dinner are heaped on a captain's chair near the bedroom door.

Out in the hallway I call his name again, even though nothing seems to be moving in this quiet house. I try to think about where he might go, so upset, in such weather. Why he'd bother to come home and change his clothes. If he were going any farther than just walking distance, wouldn't he have taken his money?

The phone rings, startling me. It rings three times. I run downstairs and pick up the receiver on the fifth ring. It's Dad.

"Everything all right?" he says, over the background voices and laughter.

"Fine," I breathe.

178

"Are you coming back for dessert?"

"Later." My heart races. "His mother wants him to stay here right now."

Dad clears his throat. "Elsa McMorran is in Toronto. She left this morning."

"I'm not coming home right now, Dad. I have to stay here."

"Is Kieran . . . okay?"

"Of course."

"Everything's all right?"

"Yes. Yes. Everything's fine."

Pause. Followed by another pause, and then, "I should tell you that some rather unpleasant things are going on in that family."

He knows. I'm so scared, I don't know what to say. I don't know how much he knows, or what he knows. Or if there are still more awful things that have happened that I don't want to know about.

"Sidonie? Stay there, I'll be right over," he says, and hangs up the phone.

There's no place to go and no place to hide. The rain, coming down around the McMorrans' darkened house, hits everything in slow, heavy plops. Holding back the scratchy lace curtain on the front door window, I watch Dad leap over puddles and cross the street. I open the door, standing behind it, as he steps inside the house. He takes off his shoes and beige trench coat. Flicks on the hall light. Rain drips off his bushy sand-colored eyebrows. I've wrapped my arms around myself and I don't know what to say.

He looks up the hall stairs, gingerly shakes raindrops off his coat. "Where's your young man?"

179

I shrug. Where is he, where is he? Waves of fear lap around the edges of my heart.

He hangs his coat over Elsa McMorran's pink sweater on the hall umbrella stand. I am ushered around the corner into the living room. We sit on the sofa. He reaches over and turns on a table lamp. I huddle away from him, clutching a tasseled pillow. Dad leans back, hand on his face, waiting for me to talk to him.

I say, as calmly as possible, "I have no idea where he's gone."

With equal calm, Dad says, "You think that he's gone somewhere."

"He was upset."

"Does he have any particular place he likes to go?"

"Maybe he walked up to the beach. This weather . . . I don't know."

"I'll go get the car."

30 ⟶©⟶

Our car, headlights beaming, pulls up in front of the McMorrans'. I dash out into the steady rain. The wind has picked up again, colder and harder than before. The door on the passenger's side swings open, and Phil gets out. His cigarette is soggy, hanging out of the side of his mouth. He reaches out, scoots me into the front seat, and gets in beside me. I sit between them as Dad, cursing the cold miserable rain, pulls away. The windshield wipers clap madly back and forth. We splash onto the valley road. Phil, shivering, cradles his arm along the seat behind me.

Dad has pulled on a gray fisherman's-knit sweater. I can smell the wet wool. He flicks on the car's heater and says, "Elsa McMorran came to this country with a medical degree and a beaten-up suitcase. All she had here was a widowed uncle, down East, who passed away three months after she arrived."

"Dad. Just please drive, okay?"

Phil rubs my arm. We are getting close to the boathouse trail.

Dad stares out into the rain. "Kieran must be a very intense young man. It's a bad situation with the father."

I straighten up and sit stiffly between them.

"Maybe," says Dad, "after this is over — you shouldn't see him for a while. That family has a lot of things to straighten out."

Phil's fingers, still straying along my coat sleeve, freeze.

"*They* do?" I explode. "And what about *us*, Dad? I'm *surrounded* by intense people. What am I supposed to do, crawl under the sofa so I won't have a nervous breakdown? Stop the car right now. I want out."

Dad looks gray in the gray darkness in his gray sweater. He stares sickly down the trail as we pull up. "Pretty muddy down there," he says. "We may get stuck."

"I don't need your help. Let me out."

I reach across Phil and flip open the door. Rain sweeps into the car. I crawl across him, get out, slam the door, and start walking down the trail.

The wild-looking lake, churning up foam, is an angry blackish green. My white party dress clings to my legs, drenched skirt bottom sucking air around my boot tops. The tall grasses, heavy headed with rain, sag onto the trail. Up ahead, lichen-spotted boards on the weathered boathouse seem to bulge around the rusty nails. Trees sway and creak in the gusts of wind, grazing the loosened tar-paper roofing. There is no sign of Kieran. I've never felt so helpless in my life.

I look out over the miles of gloomy shrouded water and

182

try to imagine where my mother is. I don't want her to hold me now. All I want is for her voice to somehow find me in this wind and tell me what to do, where to go.

Footsteps sound behind me, slurping over the mud. I turn, hoping. But it's Phil, alone.

He says, "Sidonie, my father is dead. I'd give anything just to have him back so we could have another chance. To be a good father and son. He was a hard man — not like your dad."

"Thanks for the speech."

He firmly turns me to face him. Water streams in rivulets from his black hair down his face. There is a tightness at the corners of his dark eyes. "Why do you think Bobbi has suffered so much?"

I glare at him. "Bobbi isn't the only one. Lots of people suffer."

"That's right. And sometimes they shove it all behind their hearts and pretend it isn't there. But it eats away all the same. Sooner or later you have to deal with it, Sidonie, with the people who are alive, or you end up walking around empty."

I leave him standing there. I run around the side of the boathouse to the front, which is angled toward the western expanse of the lake. I can see now that the door is open. We always leave it locked.

I climb onto the dock and step inside. It's very dark. I can't see a thing. We've always left a glass jar of wooden matches on a shelf inside the door. I fumble along the dirty ledge. Just as my eyes become accustomed to the dark, the jar hits the floor and rolls around on the uneven planking. I kneel down, feel around for it, and someone runs past me.

For a split second I see Kieran's long legs — his beige cotton shorts. Then, at the end of the dock, he's pulling off his jacket, kicking off his shoes. He hits the thrashing waves. He begins to swim away. I call out as I get up and start to run. He turns in the water. The dark waves topple around him.

I stop at the end of the dock and wrench off my boots, my coat. Unzipper my dress and peel that off, too. Then, in my panties and bra, I plunge feet first into the lake. Kieran flips over and swims away again, faster. I begin to swim after him. The water is warmer than it looks, but I gasp as the first wave washes over my head. Trying to swim sidestroke, the way he taught me, I pull along as fast as I can. I tell myself that he'll have to stop. He sees me. He knows I can't keep this up.

Don't think about the deep water. There's only this one thing to do. Only this one thing. He's swimming up ahead. Does he turn and see me?

I move faster. I'm tiring, fighting these waves. Kick my legs harder. Body moves upright. Reach for the bottom. Legs stretching down down toward nothing. Coming up for air. Water in my eyes. One wave after another. I can't see. Where is he now? Sinking again.

Water under the waves. Cold and quiet. Sinking lower than before. Deeper, deeper, there is no bottom. Bursting lungs. Shoot for the surface. Gagging on water. Waves thud thud thud over my head. Lake pulls me down.

Bubbles. Surface again. Screaming. Sink down, terribly down. Have to breathe. Isn't air. Cold hands. Reaching. Pulling. Which way is up? More water. Quiet. Maybe I'm dying.

184

31 ⟶◉⟶

Out of the blue blue silence comes a heartbeat. Delicate. Thin. Far away. Bubbles bead around me. The heart-sounds grow. My own, and the beating of some larger thing ahead. A twinkling, like starlight, tells me I'm near.

Suddenly, I see it, a fabulous wheel that rises in front of me. The heartbeats quicken and thud, filling me with sound. It slowly turns, jeweled with light, a terrifying blue beauty — a Ferris wheel that is wider than anything in sight. It stretches beyond the surface of the water.

Entire villages of people, maybe even the populations of towns and cities, seem to have been transported to this wheel. As it grows and expands, throbbing with blue and crystal light, the passengers laugh and talk, arms folded in their laps or dangling, carefree, as if they are on a journey and are confident that the trip will be safe and spectacular.

I shouldn't be here. But my body shoots forward. The

rocking, watery bench coming toward me is connected, like all the other benches, to the wheel. I slither behind the bar. My ride begins. I'm all alone as the wheel churns and beats upward. Three people sit in the bench above. A smiling woman in a summer dress and veiled hat is talking to a child, a dark-haired little girl with braids, whose eyes are large and shining. The man in a light-colored suit and a brown fedora stares ahead as if he's driving a car. They look like a family out for a Sunday drive.

Below me, a woman dressed in black Capri pants and a strange softly flowing shirt has the gently rocking bench all to herself. She's stretched out, one leg on the bench seat, knee crooked, chin on her hand. She turns around and smiles. I've never in my life seen her before, but she says, "Did you just get here?" and her voice is familiar.

"Who are you?" I ask.

She smiles a smaller, questioning smile. Her face is wonderfully clear — pale grayish blue eyes. Clean but messy black hair, curly and short. Full lips. I've seen those lips before. White teeth. I get this strange thought that she's someone I've known before. I should be able to call her by name. She glances to the place beside me, and I realize that someone has just sat down. She nods hello to that person, then turns around.

I feel the graceful silk of hair — not mine — and it's falling around my shoulders, and warming me up like a blanket. I start to relax.

We are moving steadily, magnificently, up and up. I look down at my hands. The crossed hands in the lap beside me are my mother's hands. I'd know them any-where. White thin fingers just like mine. She keeps them

186

to herself. Only her long hair glides comfortingly around me. She smells like my mother. Like her garden-scented perfume. Like her roses.

I don't have the courage yet to look at her face. But I know that eventually I'll have to. We are rising, rising, through water and blue light. Star-twinkling benches, thousands upon thousands, are rolling up as far below as our dazzled eyes can see.

The sound of heartbeats deafens all other sound as we break the surface of the water. And then the wheel continues sliding up into the night. Above and all around us the full moon fills up the sky, gleaming, soft and warm and hazy. Mauve clouds and hundreds upon hundreds of white pelicans skim across its surface. With small throaty cries, wings beating, they crowd past us. We could, if we wanted, reach out and touch them. At the very top of the Ferris wheel, we come to a full stop, bench swinging out into the air. The birds fly on above the moon and vanish like smoke.

Poised quietly at the top of the twinkling Ferris wheel, we look below. We're only specks in the universe. And now I turn to see Mom's face. She's gazing with joy at something I can't see. She isn't afraid.

I remember the woman just below us. A thin perfect gold chain glistens against her shirt. Her short curly hair is tucked back, showing off her pale cheek, her long neck, her small head. And now I'm absolutely sure that I shouldn't be here.

32 ⟋⊚⟍

These are the first things I remember after being hauled out of the lake. Being very cold and vomiting on the beach. Somebody coaxing Kieran to let go so they could pull his jacket around me. Blankets appearing from somewhere. Kieran crying, rocking me back and forth on the hard shale, saying, "I'm sorry," over and over as I gagged and coughed.

Dad's voice, angry and afraid. "You could have killed yourselves."

Rough wool blankets being pulled around me tight. Feeling like I was in a cocoon. Phil's voice at my ear ("You'll be fine. Breathe easy.") as Dad carried me up the trail.

Kieran darting ahead as the rain kept pelting down.

And in the warm car he held me in the backseat, and I said, "Promise you won't go back to your house, okay? Stay with me."

"I'm right here," he said against my cheek, just before the motion of the car and the heat and the smell of gasoline made me pull away and roll down the window and throw up again.

33 ⟋⊚⟍

Auntie Monique is not pleased. "It's a sin against God to try to kill yourself." She wipes my face with a warm, soapy washcloth.

Kieran, at the end of my bed, looks at his hands, then at the rug, hangs his head as if he wants to bury his face between his knees.

"Look at how many people you hurt," she says.

"He didn't hurt anybody," I tell her. "And he wasn't trying to kill himself."

"Then why does he swim out into the middle of the lake in a terrible dark storm with lightning cracking open the sky? Does this sound like a person who wants to be alive in the morning?" She looks sternly at him.

He lowers his head farther, elbows on his knees, hands in his hair. With my toes, under the covers, I find his leg, press hard three times. His eyes dart up, quickly meet mine, graze over Auntie Monique, then slide back to the rug.

190

"And you," she says to me. "You are not one bit better, going out after him like that — and you can't even swim!"

"I can swim. I do a fairly okay sidestroke."

She clucks her tongue, stands back, puts down the cloth, then goes at my hair with a towel. Roberta and Auntie Lucille lean with a kind of fascinated horror on either side of the door frame. They block my bedroom doorway. Auntie Lucille's arms are folded tight across her chic navy shift. She nervously reaches out and tucks a stray strand of Roberta's hair behind her ear. Roberta glances back and moves a little closer to her.

Lucille looks like a nun who has just been told there is no God.

"He *wasn't* trying to do *anything*," I say, glaring at my sister and my aunts. "He was upset. He took a jump in the lake. I jumped in after him."

"Very very foolish." Auntie Monique softens. "Sunday morning we'll all go to mass and ask for the Blessed Virgin's love and guidance."

"I don't go to church." Kieran sharply lifts his head. "And I've only been to a synagogue, once. My parents have both given up on God."

"Well, now. There's no reason why *you* should give up," Monique says cheerfully. "Art Barker, himself, is a lapsed Baptist." She waves around the towel. "Last Christmas Eve he attended midnight mass with me. He was very happy to go. He said it broadened his horizons." She rubs my head some more. "Do you need your mother's permission?"

"She isn't coming back until Monday." Kieran pulls off his water-sogged moccasins and disgustedly sends them scattering. "So she's out of sight and out of sound."

191

"And you're worried about her."

Kieran says nothing and sullenly hangs his head again.

"My dear, if you're worried, you should call her," says Auntie Monique. "No harm in that. Don't make things so complicated for yourself."

I sit up, lean over the covers, tuck my hand under Kieran's. He's wearing one of Dad's sweaters, a pale ash blue that has never been worn and that fits Kieran's long arms perfectly. Shale and sand pepper his feet and legs. His beige shorts are damp and muddy.

"Could you all leave?" I say. "For a while?"

"No harm in that either," says Monique. She leaves my bedside and shoos Auntie Lucille and Bobbi in front of her. The door closes gently behind them.

Kieran scoots up the bed. He's shy when he holds me. I hold him back, and he feels so wonderful that I melt against him. He smells so wonderful. His skin. His hair. I don't think I've ever loved anybody so much in my whole life. I could go crazy loving somebody this much. I want to tell him this. Instead, I say, making him look at me, "I think you're wonderful."

His eyes tear up and he turns away. "You almost died because of me. That's how wonderful I am. I was lucky to get you out in time."

I get out from under the covers and sit on the edge of the bed, moving my body right up against him. "We're both lucky," I tell him. "Don't you think? Don't you think that we both are?"

He turns his head and nuzzles my neck with a kiss. Little sparks fall all over my skin. His lips travel up and cover my mouth with soft kisses. "I'm the one who's lucky," he murmurs.

"It's a tie," I say, pulling him close.

There's a scuffle of paws at the door. It pops and then squeaks partway open. Bogie jumps onto the bed and slowly sinks between us. We try to ignore him. But then we accidentally squish him. He makes a short squawk, like a question.

We have to move slightly apart to give him some room. He settles down again, purring, into his fat Buddha position.

Kieran rubs his thumb along Bogie's forehead, stopping in midstroke. Bogie turns his moon-shaped ancient cat's eyes upward. Suddenly I see a blue Ferris wheel, and twinkling benches and a young woman who turns her head in a smile.

"Cats," says Kieran with a soft chuckle. "They're such know-it-alls."

34 ⟶ ☙

S ince when do you start telling me what to do with my life?" Roberta drops the orange juice squeezer into the sink.

"I'm not telling you what to do," Phil says with a big smile. "I'm merely suggesting what you might do. What the possibilities are."

"God," she mutters, rolling up her eyes.

"Don't swear," says Auntie Monique, her head in the refrigerator.

Phil leans over and gives Bobbi a quick scorcher of a kiss just before Auntie Monique straightens up and turns around with a cream pitcher in her hand. "Syrup?"

"On the table." Roberta can't take her eyes off Phil.

"Trust your instincts," says Phil. "The world could gain an enthusiastic researcher, or geriatric specialist, or internist, and lose a bored pediatrician. Wouldn't hurt a bit."

194

As I reach past her for a juice glass, she says, "Your hair looks like something the cat dragged in."

"Don't tell me. I couldn't find the brush."

"It's in the bathroom, right where you left it." She heaves one of her sighs.

"Oh, Roberta, dry up."

"Charmed, I'm sure."

"He's right, incidentally," I say. "You shouldn't become a pediatrician. You hate kids."

"See?" says Phil. "Even your sister agrees with me."

Auntie Monique comes roaring back from the dining room and pats my back on her way to the stove. "You sure were sawing logs. I've never heard anything like it — a young girl snoring!" She laughs. Flips three golden pancakes.

I locate a comb with three teeth missing beside the flour canister. "I was snoring? I didn't know I snored."

"Real loud. Did you have sweet dreams?" She stares into my eyes. It's Mom all over again. "You're okay now?"

"Really, I'm just fine." I drag the comb through my hair, ripping away at the snarls. "Has Kieran called yet?"

"No. But I'm sure he hasn't forgotten you." She laughs and pinches my chin. She turns back to the frying pan and lowers her head and practically talks to the pancakes. Then she straightens up and says, "Why isn't that Lucille dressed yet?"

"She already is. I heard her with Dad around by the roses side of the house."

"Then tell them, please, that breakfast is almost ready."

"Do we have enough for Kieran?"

She laughs again. "I always cook plenty."

195

As I'm leaving the kitchen, Bobbi sniffs the pancakes over Auntie Monique's shoulder. "You're spoiling us," she says. "How do you do that — make them all the same size? I can never get them to look right."

It's a cool sunny morning. The storm blew off all the clouds.

Dad and Lucille are both standing, arms folded, looking at the grass and talking seriously about something. Lucille's in teal green Jamaica shorts and a pale yellow blouse. Dad's wearing sandals over his socks. He casually waves away a bee with a freckled arm. He's never worn a wedding ring the way some men do. He'd always say, "I don't need a ring to prove I love your mother."

I wish he was wearing one now, though. Lucille stands so close. Too close. He glances up, sees me, shifts to the other foot. Lucille finishes what she was saying and smiles at me as I walk through the soggy grass toward them.

My mother's roses nod all over the place with fully opened flowers. She knew what she was doing when she planted them in this protected spot, but even though the storm didn't touch them, most are getting past their prime. I pinch off one and discover, hidden behind it, a single half-open bud with silky curved blushing petals. It's such a dark red that in places it's tinged with blue.

Dad says, "These were Eugenie's roses, Lucille. We don't cut them for bouquets. They don't last long when you cut them. Only a day or so."

"You put them in sugar," I say.

"Sugar?"

Lucille, arms folded, glances sidelong at his profile, then slowly swirls her sandaled foot through the grass.

196

"I read it somewhere, Dad. Sugar and warm water. They'll last at least a day longer. Everybody cuts roses. They're the flower of love." Some little jealous demon has crawled inside my head. I don't want to share my father with anybody, not now when I need to try to get to know him.

A veil shifts over his eyes. Suddenly the thing I just wished, I wish I could take back. Now all I can do is reach out and snap off Mom's perfect rose.

"Here," I say, slipping it, sweet and cool, into his buttonhole. Then I quickly hug him.

His arms come up to briefly rub my back. "How are you?" he asks sadly, pulling away.

"I'm fine."

"Are you? Are you really fine?"

"Yes, Dad. And how about you?"

"I'm okay. Thanks for asking. And thanks for your mother's rose."

Across the street, the neighbors are all out cleaning up their storm-strewn front yards.

Mr. and Mrs. Coates, in almost identical brown cardigan sweaters, toss fallen twigs and branches into a rusted wheelbarrow and then disappear around the side of their house.

Donina Stang's husband is home for the weekend. He has a beard, and he always wears plaid work shirts rolled up to his elbows. He's never in a hurry. Donina, barefoot, sits on their front steps, a china teacup warming her hands, and talks to him while he drags a long-handled rake around the base of their small crab apple tree.

As I walk across the street, she smiles up and waves me over. Her husband's name is Gerry, and he's five years older than she is. He has wrinkles around his eyes from, I guess, working outdoors most of the time and smiling into the sun.

Donina puts out her arm for me to sit beside her. I do, even though it wasn't her I was coming across the street to see.

"You have visitors?" she asks with an eager grin.

"Yes, Mom's sisters — my aunts."

Glancing up, she smiles at somebody over my shoulder.

I turn around and am startled to see Kieran standing right behind me. For a minute I can't catch my breath. The sun shines around him. If I were to get up right now my legs would probably wobble. I look back at Donina.

She pats my knee and stands up herself. She winks at Kieran and then walks down the steps.

Dad wears his rose all morning. In the afternoon it disappears. I find it, in the evening, just as Auntie Monique is calling us all for a late *tourtière* supper. It's standing in an eggcup on his dresser upstairs. I wonder if he remembered to put sugar in the water. There's my mother's picture. In it, she's smiling and about thirty years old or so, the way that my father will always remember her even when he's an old man.

I probably shouldn't think too much about what comes next. Come September. Or the winter. Or next summer. I guess everybody's life is full of surprises. Some are good. Some aren't.

Footsteps fall softly over the hardwood in the hallway. I turn toward the sound. It's Kieran. He stops at the bedroom door and pokes his head in, looking around.

"Did you finally get in touch with your mom?"

"Yes." He pads through the door, stops, looks for the light switch.

The switch plate is glass, hand-painted with flowers.

"What are you doing all alone in the dark?" he asks, finding the switch.

"Leave it, okay? There's still enough light. See how pretty the sky is?" I walk over and stand in front of the window.

"She's coming back on Tuesday now." Kieran comes up behind me. "Wants to ship out some more furniture. Looks like she's going to be staying on — living here."

"How do you feel about that?" I ask, carefully turning around.

"Part of me was so scared, Sidonie. But the other part actually hoped that everything would be better between them."

"Hope for one thing at a time," I say. "Really. I think you'll be okay."

His big worried eyes are full of questions.

"Bets?" I say. "Fifty bucks."

Kieran laughs. "*Fifty?* Do you know something I don't?"

He circles his arm around my neck, turning up my face as if to say something else. But instead with a sigh he brings me close, wrapping me all up in his arms and laying his cheek on the top of my head. We just stand there as he holds me for a very long time, until it seems that at least for now I can finally hold somebody back as long as I want.